Praise for *The Toymaker*

'This is an edge of the seat thriller that will stay in the
mind long after the book finishes' IRISH EXAMINER

'The story is pacy, exciting and inventive with
strong and interesting characters' GUARDIAN

The Toymaker is refreshingly readable with some downright
creepy moments . . . The ending is as dark as the story deserves
. . . you'll definitely be left wanting more'
SFX

'This is a world of shadows and terror told with the
utmost conviction. A remarkable debut novel' CAROUSEL

This is a new, strong and distinctive voice. More please'
BOOKS FOR KEEPS

'Classic tale for long winter nights' BOOKSELLER

'antastic story set in an imaginary world' SCHOOL LIBRARIAN

'*The Toymaker* is fast paced and beautifully written'
JUNIOR EDUCATION PLUS

For Lizzie, Jack, Alice and Bea,
who all came to sea in the sieve.

THE
TOYMAKER

Jeremy de Quidt
With illustrations by Gary Blythe

David Fickling Books
OXFORD · NEW YORK
31 Beaumont Street
Oxford OX1 2NP, UK

THE TOYMAKER
A DAVID FICKLING BOOK 978 1 849 92004 9

First published in Great Britain by David Fickling Books,
a division of Random House Children's Books
A Random House Group Company

Hardback edition published 2008
This edition published 2010

1 3 5 7 9 10 8 6 4 2

Text copyright © Jeremy de Quidt, 2008
Interior illustrations copyright © Gary Blythe, 2008

The Random House Group Limited supports the Forest Stewardship
Council (FSC), the leading international forest certification organization.
All our titles that are printed on Greenpeace-approved FSC-certified paper
carry the FSC logo. Our paper procurement policy can be found at
www.rbooks.co.uk/environment.

Set in 12/16pt New Baskerville

DAVID FICKLING BOOKS
31 Beaumont Street, Oxford, OX1 2NP

www.**kids**at**random**house.co.uk
www.**rbooks**.co.uk

Addresses for companies within The Random House Group Limited
can be found at: www.randomhouse.co.uk/offices.htm

THE RANDOM HOUSE GROUP Limited Reg. No. 954009

A CIP catalogue record for this book is available from the British Library.

Printed in the UK by CPI Bookmarque, Croydon, CR0 4TD

Contents

remarkable toys that any man ever made. He made them, you know. He didn't buy them and sell them on like some cheap shopkeeper. No. He made them. Small moving men and women, and carts and horses, and birds and dogs and cats and fish – all manner of quite astonishing things. They each had their own key – no one Menschenmacher key fitted them all, other than the one that Menschenmacher himself kept on a chain about his waistcoat. No. You had to have the exact key for the exact toy if you were to make it work. And work they did. The keys were remarkable enough in themselves, fine silver and bronze – and small. So small. You had to pinch them tight between your nails to hold them. Each toy had a hidden place for its key. Fit it in and turn and turn, and then stand back and wonder.

For a moment nothing would happen and then – I swear it is true – the eyes in its head would turn and look at you as if to say, *Well, what shall it be today?* Then the toy would move and you would never know what it would do next. It never did the same thing twice. If it was a horse, it might rear up and gallop, and you would have to catch it quickly before it jumped off the tabletop; a woman in her fine court dress might curtsey and dance in slow graceful turns, or a soldier or guard might lower his pike and stab at your hand if you didn't snatch it away in time. And their eyes *did* move, I tell you. I have tried it. I wound one once – it was not mine but I had the chance – and letting it go, I stood away and watched those small bright eyes turn until they found me, which was unnerving. If I were not as sensible as I am, I might say that they, or something in them, was alive. But of course they were not. They were toys. When their spring had wound down, they would stop quite still and not move again from now until Christmas unless you put the key in again and wound it up.

They were very expensive. All sorts of wealth and nobility bought them. You sometimes saw the grand carriages stop in Frausisstrasse and the coachman descend and open the door. Then down they would step in their rich clothes, and pass through the wooden arch that led to the small dead-end where Menschenmacher had his shop. And then they would come back carrying a small box looped with a red ribbon and you would know what was in it.

Menschenmacher would not let anyone watch him make a toy, though his workbench was there to see if you went into his shop. Each day at four o'clock he would close the shutters and pull down the blinds, and that is all that the world would see of him until the next morning when he opened them again. There were tools on the bench, a small lathe for cutting the minute cogs and wheels that filled his toys – so minute that above them there was a large glass to magnify the work so that he could see it all. And screwdrivers no bigger than pins and soldering irons no larger than a needle. That is what he used, but you would not see him do it. When the shop was shut – that was when Menschenmacher worked.

People were afraid of him. That's strange, isn't it – to be afraid of a toymaker? But they were. It was that same feeling of fear that steals up on you in the night when you are alone. It doesn't need any words. It was wrapped around Menschenmacher like a cloak, as though when he looked at the people who came into his shop, he already knew just what each one of them feared most in the world. Knew it, and could make it happen if he chose.

No.

They were glad to be out through the door again and into the busy street, the wonderful toy with its red ribboned box in their hand. They would never have gone in had it not been for that.

Now let me tell you something that no one else

knew. That bench by the workshop window – he had it there to catch the daylight – that wasn't his only workbench.

He had another.

If you went into his shop, the counter was to the right, so, the bench to the left by the window, and the small winding stair over in the corner. At the bottom of the stair was a cupboard. Well, I say a cupboard, but it was not much more than a thick green velvet curtain on a pole that he pulled across to cover up the boxes and wrapping and small things that he needed. You could see them because the curtain was always a little bit open.

And that was the trick.

You thought that it was just a curtain and a cupboard because you could see that that was all there was. But it wasn't. When the shutters were closed and the blinds pulled down, Menschenmacher would draw the curtain back, move the empty boxes away and, finding the key, that small key upon his waistcoat that would fit all the toys, slip it into a crack in the wall – no, not a crack, though it might look like one. A lock. He turned the key and pushed, and the wall opened. He always looked to see that there was no one behind him, then he drew the curtain shut and, going through the wall, closed and locked it.

And that is where his other workplace was.

What good is a toy that you wind up? It will wind down and stop. Clever though the toys were that he sold from his shop, they were lumps of metal and clay compared to the things he made down there. What good is a toy that will wind down? What if you could put a heart in one? A real heart. One that beats and beats and doesn't stop. What couldn't you do if you could make a toy like that?

Menschenmacher would sit at his bench and look at his tools with his pale green eyes and think on it.

At first he had no success. He would set small wicker traps in the little dark yard behind the shop. He sprinkled the ground with crumbs and laid the trap above them – a basket propped up with a stick. Then he would watch until a sparrow or a starling came down and, careless of the trap, pecked up the crumbs, and he would pull on a string, the stick would fall, and down the basket would come. He had tiny cages for them – they were no use to him dead. The cages lined the wall of the workshop. The birds sat and looked out into the room. A hundred black beady eyes. And he would work at his bench until he was ready, with the half-made toy open before him. Then he would take a sparrow from a cage and, with a quick knife, take out its heart, still beating, and try to fit it into the toy, carefully joining the tiny cogs and wheels so that the fluttering heart might make them move. But he could not make it work.

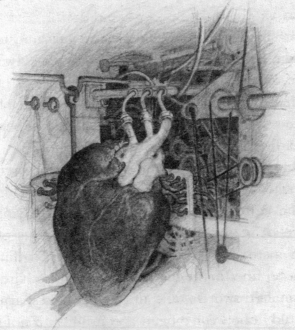

There was something that could not be made to work. The toy would lie there as lifeless as the sparrow, and in a fury he would throw them both into the fire and watch them burn.

Sometimes, even though he worked so fast, the heart would stop beating before he even placed it in the toy. But at other times it would beat on, just for a moment, and the limbs of the toy would jerk and the eyelids flicker as though about to open, but then the heart would stop and there was no starting it again.

The more he tried, the nearer he came to the answer, until one day he knew what it was. It was the knife. In cutting out the heart of the sparrow he was cutting out its life too. What he needed was a blade so fine, so sharp, so minute, that it could fit between a heart and its life and not sever the two.

That is what he set himself to make, when the town clocks struck four and the shutters were drawn. In the light of the fire and his brightest lamp, all reflected in the hundred black beady eyes of the birds in the cages on the wall, he tried to make a blade so fine that it could not be seen, so hard that a tempered sword would not break it, so sharp that it could fit between a heart and its life and not sever the two.

When he made it, he set it into an ivory handle. It was a blade as cruel as frost, so thin that though you might see the ivory handle, try as you might you could not see the blade.

Nothing had ever been made before that was as sharp as that.

When Menschenmacher slid the blade into a sparrow's breast, it looked at him with momentarily puzzled eyes. It never knew that its heart had been taken. Menschenmacher set the tiny thing, still beating, into the open toy upon his bench and joined the wheels and cogs, the minute gears and pins. Then he stood back and waited as the heart beat on.

The toy moved its limbs as might a man waking.

And opened its eyes.

PART ONE
The Conjuror's Boy

1

The Man with the White Face

As circuses go, it was not very large. It hardly
warranted the name at all. 'Travelling show' was
more like it. There were only two carts. The wood of
their sides was rotten – no amount of bright paint
could hide that – and there were only four horses to
pull them both, two to each cart. They were old
horses, bone thin. How they managed to pull those
heavy carts through the winter mud I don't know,
but horses do that. They keep on going while there
is breath in their body. They have big hearts, horses.
Did you know you can ride a horse to death? You
really can. It won't complain. It will keep going and
keep going until it drops dead of exhaustion
beneath you. Then you have to walk. So if you have
any sense, you don't do that. You rest the horse when
it needs it, and you have to decide when that is

because the horse can't tell you. It will just carry on and on until it drops dead. Imagine that.

There had once been two more horses than there were now. They would walk behind the second cart on a long rope and be changed over when the others needed a rest. But these were wild times and there were no safe roads. The thick woods hid things – wolves as well as men. It was the wolves that got them. Just before dark they came out of the woods without a sound – silent and hungry and big. They had the two following horses down before anyone could do a thing: the horses were screaming and plunging at their ropes but the wolves just sank their teeth in and wouldn't let go even though the halters were still tied and the cart was dragging the wolves and the kicking horses along the ground. So the circus men cut the ropes and the two carts went on as fast as they could, leaving those two horses to the wolves. There was a small lamp in each cart and by its light the people could just see the fear on each other's faces as the wolves killed the screaming horses, and then everything was quiet except for their own scared breathing and the creaking of the carts as they continued on their way.

The first cart carried everything that was needed:

the food, the faded costumes, the props. With that cart went the owner, Lutsmann, and his painted wife, Anna-Maria. He said that this arrangement allowed him to check that everything was always to hand when it was needed, but everyone knew that it was because Lutsmann thought they would steal things if he put them in the second cart. That's the kind of man he was. He thought that people would steal from him because he never missed a chance to steal from them. He stole from them in the thin food he gave them; he stole from them in the wages he never paid and in the promises he never kept. But they had nowhere else to go. They were people who had once wanted nothing more from life than to juggle and dance, breathe great gouts of fire, turn somersaults and lift enormous weights, but they had never been quite good enough at their art to find a place in a proper show. When they were taken on by Lutsmann, they thought that it was at least something – a start. Only then did they realize that this was all they would ever have, and that all their dreams and their hopes had gone. They had nothing left but Lutsmann's Travelling Circus. It is a terrible thing to have no dreams, no hopes. So, in many ways, as well as owning the carts, Lutsmann owned them too.

His wife, Anna-Maria, was a vicious woman. She considered herself a great beauty. Maybe she had been once. She painted her face thick with make-up. Rouged her cheeks, blacked her eyelashes, reddened her lips – dark as blood. She carried herself with a haughty highness and had a riding crop with which she laid about her when her temper was raised. Lutsmann called her crooningly 'my dove', 'my apple'. She called him simply 'Lutsmann', and he jumped when she spoke.

But what of the performers? You might expect that if they weren't looked after by Lutsmann, then at least they looked after each other. But you'd be wrong. They were petty and vindictive. Maybe that is really why they found themselves where they were. They were that sort of person: Lutsmann's show was just the lowest sink into which they had all fallen. Perhaps they would have been the same anywhere. Or maybe they could have been better if the world had been better to them. That is a very hard question. It's not one that I know the answer to. There was a strongman, a fire-eater, a tightrope-walker, a juggler and dancer, a lady who could bend her body in quite impossible ways, a conjuror and a boy. And mind. He couldn't remember them easily – not that he really wanted to. He had to make do with things as they were, because he had no other choice.

Now, there were two important things that he knew: the first was that Gustav was his grandfather; the second, well, that was something that he almost knew. It was a great secret that Gustav was going to tell him one day. Once, when Gustav had been drunk – often he was very drunk – he had told Mathias that he knew a secret. A secret that would make Gustav rich beyond all dreams. A secret so big that there were men who would kill him rather than have it told. When Gustav was sober again, Mathias asked him what the secret was and Gustav's eyes had narrowed because he knew he'd said too much to the boy. 'You must never tell,' he told Mathias. 'If you are a good boy and do all that I say, one day I will tell you what it is, the secret that only I know.' And he had put his finger to Mathias's lips and then to his own. 'One day, if you are always a good boy.'

The secret was why – and this is the strange thing that I was going to tell you – Gustav had painted his face quite white. He never took the paint off. Ever. What better disguise than a face as white as a corpse? What better place to hide than a travelling circus, what better companion than his grandson? How could such a person know anything?

When Gustav joined Lutsmann's circus, he had actually been a very good conjuror. If people do not understand how a thing is done, they are prepared to believe that it might, just might, be magic. If I were to open my hand and, where a moment before there had been nothing there was now a bird, you might not understand how I had done it but you would guess that somehow I had put it there. But if I were to ask you to turn *your* hand over, peel back your fingers and in your palm was a bird – now how could that have got there? That is what Gustav could do. That and many more things too. He could make a tight scarf appear around a man's throat if he had called out from the crowd and made him angry. 'Take care,' he would say, 'or next time I will make it a rope.'

It was not magic, but how could it have been done?

He was a finer conjuror than Lutsmann could ever have expected to find, and Lutsmann snapped him up having seen only part of what Gustav could do. He took him, child and all, and no questions were ever asked. But Lutsmann knew a man with a past when he saw one. What did it matter to him? He had a conjuror and Gustav had somewhere to hide – what more did either want?

Well, I'll tell you what Lutsmann wanted – what Anna-Maria wanted. They wanted to know what it was that Gustav had to hide. Why else would a man like him have come to them? Why else would he never show his real face?

This was the life that Mathias led in the circus. Preparing the things the performers would need. Helping them dress and undress, and never any thanks given. Estella, the lady contortionist, was the worst. Mathias would avoid her when he could. Sometimes he couldn't. She would call him 'my pretty boy' and put her hand beneath his chin as though to pet him, but instead she would dig her finger hard into the top of his throat so that he hung there upon her nail as if upon a single spike. 'My pretty boy,' she would say, and then her voice was like a cat snagging silk with its claws. He fetched their water, he cleaned and mended, and did all the things that a child shouldn't have to do. But he had no choice. There was no one else to look after him.

When they came to a place that was large enough for a show, Lutsmann would stop the brightly painted carts. The side of the second cart would be lowered so as to make a stage, and there Lutsmann would stand in his fine clothes, black boots and red coat, shouting until he had a crowd. Beside him stood the man who ate fire. He would thrust a lighted torch into his mouth and blow out a jet of flame that lit a twist of straw Lutsmann held in his hand. He could swallow swords too. He could put five of them down his throat at once, one after the other. While this was happening Gustav would be on the stage too, whirling cards out of his hands in ribbons and drawing them back in, spreading them like fans, making them loop the loop. Estella would fold her body around and sit on her own head, and all the time Lutsmann would be shouting and beating a drum while Anna-Maria went amongst the crowd and sold tickets for the show. For this wasn't the show itself; this was just enough to make people want to come. The real show would only happen when the light faded and the burning torches were lit. Then everything was in shadow, and in the flickering light people didn't see the cheaply painted carts; they saw what they wanted to believe.

In the light of the flaming torches, Lutsmann would introduce each act before it came on. The

strongman would come first. Like most circus shows, not all was what it seemed. While he was showing his muscles to the crowd, it was Mathias's job to crawl into a secret space beneath the cart and, at the right moment, hook to an iron bar beneath the floor the huge weights the strongman was to lift, so that when Lutsmann called the young men up to try their luck, they couldn't move them an inch. He knew when to unhook them too, so that the strongman, face red with pretended effort, could sail them above his head to the gasps of the crowd.

Then Estella's turn would come. There was nothing fake about her. She would bend and twist her thin body, and the village men would stare at her, wide-eyed and greedy, until their wives made them look away. Then came the fire-eater, the juggler and the tightrope walker, and then, last of all, Gustav. Mathias would watch the faces in the crowd as they stared open-mouthed as Gustav pulled flags from the air and sent glowing balls floating just out of reach over their heads. What Mathias never saw though was how, from behind his white face, Gustav carefully searched the faces in the crowd for one that he knew.

It puzzled Mathias that Gustav never showed the crowd what he could really do. It was much more than they ever saw. Sometimes Gustav could be kind, though it was strange when he was – he would show Mathias a trick to stop his tears. 'Look,' he would say, and then he would do something remarkable – like finding the bird in Mathias's hand, or making cold blue flames burn on the tip of each of his fingers. When he did those tricks, the air would fill with a scent, like honey and resin. It clung to Gustav's clothes afterwards, but Mathias never knew what it was, and Gustav would never tell him.

And that is how it was.

But then things got worse. Mathias saw that his grandfather was becoming absent-minded. He was vague on the stage. He mistimed his tricks now and then, even dropped things, which was unheard of. At night Gustav would twitch and turn in his bed, and if Mathias got up – there was no toilet in the cart – Gustav would catch hold of him as though he were a thief and stare at him for minutes on end in the darkness, wanting to know, over and over, if the daylight was coming. Sometimes he didn't know who Mathias was or why he was there, and then he got angry, accusing him of trying to steal his secret. For as long as Mathias could remember, Gustav had slept with a pistol beneath his pillow. But one night, when he was raving like that, Gustav put it to the side of Mathias's head and held it there in trembling silence. It was the longest moment Mathias had ever known.

In the morning, when Gustav was himself again and weeping floods of self-pitying tears, Mathias threw the pistol into the long grass and Gustav never noticed it had gone, or if he did, he said nothing.

There was no medicine that made any difference. Gustav tried several – little red bottles that he would tip down his throat in one swallow, or mix in a small tumbler with wine. It got so that he couldn't do his act any more. He started to tremble and his words were hard to understand. He forgot things halfway through, and the crowd would hiss and laugh at him as the tricks dropped from his hands. But for all that had happened, Mathias still felt tears of rage behind his eyes when they laughed at the feeble man with the white face, because when all was said and done, he was his grandfather. But that became the act. Lutsmann saw to it. The others didn't want Gustav any more – he was just an extra mouth to feed – but Lutsmann did. 'I am doing you a favour,' he would say in his fat, greasy voice, putting his arm around Mathias. 'Let the people laugh at him and we will still feed you.' Then he would thumb his large nose. 'Maybe one day you will be able to do something to repay us?'

Mathias knew what that was. Lutsmann wanted to know what Gustav's secret was. Once, Mathias had surprised Anna-Maria going through Gustav's bags. She said she had been tidying up – 'Such a mess.' But she needn't have said anything and Mathias

31

knew that she had been looking for something, even if she didn't know exactly what it was. They weren't afraid of Gustav now that he was feeble and dribbled and couldn't do the trick of putting a rope around their neck. So Mathias looked after him, and so far as a boy was able he protected him too, because he was his grandfather.

And that is the kind of boy that Mathias was.

Then came the day of the wolves and the horses. The circus travelled on and set up in the next market square. The cart they travelled in was emptied out as usual and the stage set. When it came to Gustav's turn, he stood looking down at the sea of grinning faces, not sure what it was that he was supposed to do next. Mathias looked away as he always did because he knew what was going to happen and he couldn't bear to watch it. But as he turned away, he saw in the crowd a man with a silver-topped cane. It was the cane that he saw first – the top of it caught the light of the flaring torches that lit the stage. It struck Mathias as odd because in the last town there had been a cane like that too; it had gleamed then. And then he looked at the man who held it, and realized that it was the same man as well. And that struck him as odd, because people wouldn't come to see the same show twice. Certainly not follow it from one town to the next. But there he was, Mathias was sure. He was standing near the back, his eyes intently watching the man on the stage. Then Gustav saw him too. He stopped stock-still, staring at the man with the silver-topped cane. He started to dribble; he looked wildly from side to side as though he were trying to find somewhere to run to, but as he lurched forward his knees caught the side of the cart and he pitched head first over the edge of the stage and onto the hard stone beneath.

2
The Man with the Silver-topped Cane

The crowd let out a whoop of delight as Gustav fell from the stage. One or two of the men rushed forward and tried to pick him up and push him back on, but his body was as limp as a rag doll, and then, by the light of the flaring torches, they saw that they had blood on their hands. Gustav's hair was thick with it. It made thin black ropes down the white of his face. They put him down on the ground and stepped back. Others jostled to get a better look. Mathias couldn't get through. A man was elbowing his way through the crowd. Mathias grabbed hold of his coat and, holding tight, was pulled through. It was the man with the silver-topped cane. He was shouting, 'Let me through!' and pushing the gawping people aside.

When he got to the cart, he knelt down beside

Gustav and laid his ear to the old man's chest to listen. The whole dreadful scene was lit by the flaring torches. Mathias saw it all – the eager faces of the crowd in the flickering shadows, the tall man with his head upon Gustav's chest, the lines of blood on the chalk-white face.

'He's alive,' the man said. He pointed to the two nearest men in the crowd. 'You and you. Carry him.'

The cart had been set up in the large square in front of the coaching inn. It was always the best place. The two men carried Gustav's limp body like a sack of flour between them. The man with the silver-topped cane went in front. As they came into the courtyard of the inn, he called out, 'We have a man hurt!'

The tapster in his thick leather apron looked down at Gustav and at the small common crowd that had trailed along to watch. There was no money to be had there. He pointed to one of the empty stables.

'I'll pay,' said the man with the cane.

The tapster looked at Gustav again and shook his head. 'He can die in there just as well as in any of my beds.'

The man with the cane didn't argue. They carried

Gustav through an open stable door and laid him down in the deep, dirty straw. Someone lit a lamp.

'Shouldn't we get a doctor?' said Mathias.

It was only then that the man noticed him. He must have thought that he was just one of the crowd come to stare. Some of them had pushed into the stable. Those who couldn't actually get in peered round the open door.

'He's my grandfather,' Mathias said.

The man looked at him with sudden, new attention. 'You needn't worry, boy,' he said in a hard, cold voice. 'I am a doctor. Can you run?'

Mathias nodded.

'Go and tell your circus man what has happened. Then get me clean water and a cloth. Go! Be quick! And you' – he spoke to the men who had carried Gustav in – 'keep this rabble out!'

He dropped money into the hand of the first man. They didn't need any more telling. They were both big men, and with pushes and punches they emptied the stable in a moment. The man with the cane closed the door behind them, then turned to where Gustav lay unconscious in the deep straw.

'So,' he said. 'Let us see if you really are who I think you are.'

Mathias ran as fast as he could to find Lutsmann. Lutsmann had already heard what had happened but his concerns were very different from those of Mathias. He was standing behind the cart that held the clothes, arguing with Estella. He wanted her to go onto the stage again. She was standing with her hands on her snake-thin hips. She had done her part, she said. She would only do more – and she held her hand out like someone rubbing money – if he paid her. Lutsmann's face was scarlet. The people who had not trailed after Gustav to the inn but had waited instead for another act were getting impatient. Mathias could hear them whistling and throwing stones onto the empty stage. All of a sudden Anna-Maria stepped out from the shadows. Mathias had not known that she was even there. She pushed past Lutsmann and gave Estella such a slap across the face with her bare hand that it must have loosened the woman's teeth. Estella shrieked and, with fingers like claws, flew at Anna-Maria, who cut at her with her riding crop. The two women grabbed hold of each other's hair and, pulling and scratching, fell to the ground. Lutsmann tried to drag them apart. Estella bit him hard on the hand. He yelled and kicked her. There was no stopping them. Mathias ran back to the inn to get the water, cursing himself for having wasted time.

When he opened the door of the stable, he saw that the man with the cane had taken Gustav's coat off him and had it in his hands. All the pockets had been turned inside out and emptied onto the straw.

'What are you doing?' said Mathias, but the man didn't answer. He tossed the coat onto the ground.

'Bring the water here,' he said.

Mathias put the bowl down beside Gustav's head. The man took the cloth and, wetting it, began to wash the blood from Gustav's forehead and chin. But he was rubbing so hard. Then Mathias realized that he wasn't washing the blood away at all. He was washing the white paint off Gustav's face. It was a face that Mathias had never seen before. It seemed wrong for this stranger to be uncovering it. He pushed at him and tried to take the cloth away, but the man was too strong. He shoved Mathias away into the straw. When Mathias tried again, the man hit him with the back of his hand, sending him sprawling into the corner and making his nose bleed. Then the man stood up and lifted the lamp from where it had been hung on a hook. He bent over Gustav and looked at the washed face as though for something that he was expecting to find. Mathias crept forward.

Where the white paint had been washed off, Gustav's bare face was deathly pale, save for one cheek, which had a large red stain – a birth mark – like port wine. It was as big as a hand. Mathias had never seen it before, never known it was even there.

The man turned to him. 'He is your grandfather, you say?'

Mathias nodded.

The man settled himself in the straw, beside Gustav's head. 'Conjuror,' he said. 'Can you hear?'

Gustav didn't move. The man shook him.

'Can you hear?'

But Gustav lay quite still.

'Stay with him,' said the man and, picking up his cane, went out of the stable.

It was so cold. Mathias took Gustav's coat and spread it over the motionless man, and as he did so, Gustav suddenly opened his eyes wide. His lips moved. Mathias bent down to try to hear what he was saying, but he couldn't make out the words. Gustav's fingers were pulling at the coat. Mathias folded it around him. But Gustav's fingers kept pulling at it. Mathias realized that he was trying to pull the coat to him.

'The coat?' Mathias said. 'You want the coat?'

Gustav didn't answer. The pockets had already been turned inside out; even the lining had been slit with a blade and pulled through. But Gustav's fingers were working at the lapel by the collar. Mathias took the coat from him. Beneath the thick cloth he could feel something – a small hard lump. He looked quickly over his shoulder lest the man return, then began picking at the stitching with his fingernails, but he couldn't break it. He put it in his mouth and ground his teeth against it. The cloth tasted dirty and bitter, but his teeth made a small hole. He chewed it larger then, spitting the threads out, pulled through the hole a tight roll of paper.

He looked over his shoulder again. 'Is this it?'

For the first time Gustav's eyes seemed to focus. With trembling fingers he took the paper and, opening his mouth, put it in and tried to chew, but the effort was simply too much. His eyes drooped closed and his head lolled back onto the straw. Mathias put his ear to the old man's chest but there was no sound. Gustav was dead.

There were people still outside. One of them pushed open the door to see what had happened. In ones and twos they came in and looked down at the dead man, then, bored by what they saw, wandered away. Mathias's nose was still bleeding, but he didn't want to touch the water or the cloth, which were milky white with the paint from Gustav's face, so he wiped his nose on his sleeve and sat in the straw and cried.

He didn't know how long he cried for, but the people had gone. He sat looking at his dead grandfather, at the strange, hollow face, not knowing what to do next. Then he remembered the piece of paper. Very gently, he prised open Gustav's mouth. The paper was still there on the back of his wet tongue.

3
Boy and Belongings

Mathias didn't know whether Anna-Maria had seen what he'd done. He took his hand quickly out of his pocket.

'Get up,' she said.

Her words were always clipped; they never offered any choice. She expected people to do what she told them. If they didn't, they learned the consequences pretty quickly and by the next time they knew better. Mathias stood up, still unsure whether she had seen him put the piece of paper in his pocket. But she wasn't looking at him. She was looking at Gustav's face and coat.

'Who did this?' she demanded.

'The man who was here,' said Mathias.

Her face filled with a look of greed and suspicion. 'Did he find anything?'

Mathias shook his head. 'I don't know what he was looking for,' he said, but in his own mind he thought he knew.

Anna-Maria put her face very close to his. He could smell the perfumed powder on her skin.

'You'd better be right,' she said, and her voice was cruel.

She gripped Mathias's arm and pulled him across the market square towards where the stage cart stood. Its big, heavy curtains were drawn shut. The audience had drifted away and the torches had been put out. Mathias could smell the wisps of oily smoke in the air. In the dark Anna-Maria led him up the wooden steps of Lutsmann's cart. Beneath the crack of its door he could see the glimmer of light.

'My dove,' said Lutsmann, in a voice that was greasy and false, as Anna-Maria opened the door. 'Have you found the poor dear boy?'

Anna-Maria, who the moment before had been pulling at Mathias, gripping his arm so tightly that it hurt, now gently ushered him in, brushing his hair tidy with her fingers as though he were the very apple of her eye.

'I found him by poor Gustav's body,' she said silkily and looked down at Mathias sorrowfully. 'The lamb.'

But Mathias didn't look at her. His eyes were fixed on the other man in the cart, on his hat and silver-topped cane. He was sitting opposite Lutsmann at the small table. In the bright lamplight, Mathias was able to have a good look at him for the first time. He had dark, hard eyes in a face that was quite round, pudgy, like a small moon. There was an ill-disguised contempt for Lutsmann on his face, a not believing a word of the charade that was being played out before him.

'This is Doctor . . .'

'Leiter,' said the man.

'Yes,' said Lutsmann, as though he in turn doubted that it was the man's name at all. 'Doctor Leiter has an offer to make to you, Mathias. A very generous offer.'

Lutsmann's eyes strayed to the table. Mathias noticed for the first time a small leather pouch, there by Lutsmann's hand. He didn't have to guess very hard what it might contain.

'He has need of an assistant and has offered to take you on' – here Lutsmann put his hand on his heart and shook his head mournfully – 'now that Gustav is no more.'

'Oh, Gustav!' sobbed Anna-Maria.

She lifted her hanky to her face, but Mathias saw that from behind the lace her eyes were watching Dr Leiter as carefully as a stalking cat.

'The choice is yours, Mathias,' said Lutsmann. 'This circus is your family and your home.' He turned to the other man. 'We love him as if he were our own dear son,' he explained. 'But, Mathias, you must think on your future.'

He's going to sell me, thought Mathias.

He looked again at the fat purse full of money. Anna-Maria's hand rested lightly on his shoulder, and though that touch could have been mistaken for something more kindly, Mathias knew exactly what it meant – it meant, *Shut up and don't say a word.*

He stood there, looking from Lutsmann's greedy face to the hard eyes of Dr Leiter. His nose still hurt from where the doctor had hit him.

'See!' said Lutsmann grandly. 'The boy is speechless, no doubt with gratitude.'

'Quite,' said Leiter coldly. He looked at Mathias, then at Lutsmann. 'The price includes all his things and those of the grandfather too.'

Lutsmann pulled a new face, thoughtful. 'I wonder if we should not reconsider that,' he said.

'They are after all valuable props and—'

Almost carelessly, while Lutsmann had been speaking, Leiter had picked up his cane. Now he twisted the silver top. It parted from the rest of the stick, just an inch, but enough to show Lutsmann the hard, bright steel of the long blade that was hidden inside. Lutsmann swallowed.

'The price we agreed was for everything, circus man,' said Dr Leiter. 'Boy. Baggage. Belongings. What was the grandfather's is now the boy's.'

'Of c-course,' said Lutsmann, stammering over the words. 'But I was just thinking—'

'Don't,' said Leiter. 'Thinking can have such unfortunate consequences.'

He stood up. 'The boy can show me everything. He will know what can be taken and what cannot.'

With that, he stepped across to the door and, pushing Mathias in front of him, opened it and went down the steps into the cold darkness.

Anna-Maria closed the door but left enough of a crack to spy through. She pressed her eye up against it.

'What a price!' crowed Lutsmann, clapping the leather purse between his hands. 'What a fool he was. Did you see how I nearly even got a bit more too.'

'Ssshhh!' hissed Anna-Maria. 'I want to see what they do.'

'Let the fool go. He has left his money.'

'You're the fool! Idiot!' she hissed. 'He wasn't paying for the boy. He was paying for something else. He searched Gustav's coat. Stripped the lining bare. Now he wants his things. Whatever it is has got to be in there.'

'Then why did you let me sell them, my plum?' said Lutsmann stupidly.

'It was you who sold them, you fool.' Without taking her eye from the crack in the door, Anna-Maria aimed a kick at Lutsmann. 'I couldn't stop you. I said sell the boy, not the old goat's things. Now shut up and let me watch.'

She could see the door of the stage cart and, by the spill of light from inside it, the shapes of Mathias and the doctor climbing the ladder at the back.

Mathias was too frightened to think as he stepped down into the dark. It was so cold. He put his hands in his pockets, and at once his fingers touched and closed around the little roll of paper. He looked

onto the floorboards. Then he spread it about with his foot as though looking for something that might have been hidden. But there was nothing.

'Get the bags,' he said.

Mathias picked up the bags.

'And there is nothing else?'

Mathias shook his head.

'No secret place?'

He shook his head again.

'Where did he keep his money?'

'He had no money.'

Gustav never had any, or if he had, Mathias had never seen it.

Leiter slid the blade back into his cane. He turned the lamp down again, then opened the door.

'Where are we going?' Mathias asked.

'On a short journey,' said Leiter.

The bags were awkward to carry. By the time Mathias was at the foot of the steps Leiter was already a dimly seen shape in the darkness.

'What about my grandfather?' he called.

The shape stopped.

'If you do not come now, boy,' said Leiter, 'something very bad will happen to you.'

There was a movement in the darkness behind

Mathias. He saw it from the corner of his eye. He turned round, but he could see nothing. There was something there though. He could hear it. It was dragging sharp fingernails along the side of the wooden cart. He felt suddenly alone and very frightened. He looked quickly across to the lights of the tavern. They were too far to run to.

'Very bad,' breathed a whisper close beside his ear.

He whirled round but there was still no one there. Something picked at his coat sleeve. He tried to brush it away. He could feel a whimper rising in his throat.

'Come along, boy,' called Leiter from the dark.

Mathias had no choice. He picked up the bags and, not daring to look behind him, started to run as fast as he could after the disappearing shape of Dr Leiter.

4

The Road Through the Wood

Lamps burned at the corners of the narrow streets. It was late now and quite dark. There were no other people to see them. Leiter walked so fast that his long black coat-tails trailed out behind him. Mathias tried to keep up, but it was hard. The bags were heavy and kept catching him in the same place behind his knee so that it blistered and scraped. If he stopped for breath, he thought he could hear other steps in the dark behind him stop and wait. When he started, they started again. Only once did he dare glance behind him. He snatched a look over his shoulder and saw a shape, small as a child, but much broader, wider, slip out of the lamplight and back into the shadow.

At last Leiter stopped. There was a low black carriage waiting beneath one of the corner lamps.

Its two horses stood strangely still – not shaking their heads or chewing on their bits. They were immobile, like statues of horses. They didn't even turn their heads when Leiter opened the carriage door and climbed in. Mathias put the bags down on the street beside the carriage and hesitated. He didn't want to get in, but when he looked back, there was the shape again, flitting from shadow to shadow between the lamps in a low, scuttling run. It was getting nearer. Leiter leaned forward and, crooking his finger through the open door, beckoned to Mathias.

'Get in, boy,' he said. 'Believe me, you really do not want to let him catch you.'

Mathias scrambled through the door and onto the hard leather seat beside Leiter.

'And the bags,' said Leiter. 'Don't forget the bags.'

Mathias had left them on the ground outside.

'You'd better be quick, mind,' said Leiter.

Mathias scrambled down from the carriage, grabbed the bags and pushed them in through the door, but they wedged halfway. He could see the shape – it was in the shadows by the horses. He gave the bags one last desperate heave and, with a sound of tearing canvas, they shot through the door like a cork from a bottle. Leiter grabbed him by the scruff of his neck and pulled him in after them, then someone slammed the door from outside.

'Good,' said Leiter.

The carriage rocked on its springs as though someone had climbed onto the driver's bench and was picking up the reins. Leiter rapped sharply on the roof with the silver top of his cane. The carriage jolted and began to move.

Back in the circus cart, Anna-Maria held the lamp.

'Try that one again,' she said.

Lutsmann was on his hands and knees, opening the chests and boxes that held the circus things.

'There is nothing of Gustav's here,' he said.

'Look again, fool!'

'There is not, my lamb. It has all gone.'

The straw from the mattress was spread across the floor. Under Anna-Maria's direction Lutsmann had emptied everything else from the chests on top of it.

'Fool!' she said again. 'Ass!'

She kicked his fat behind hard with her pointed shoe, so that he fell forward into one of the open boxes.

'What was he looking for?'

'I don't know, my dove,' said Lutsmann, emerging

from the box, pulling pieces of straw from his mouth and hair.

'What could it have been?'

'We'll never know now, my cake-bread,' said Lutsmann.

Anna-Maria bent down and, grabbing him by his scarf, twisted it tight. 'Oh, yes we will,' she hissed through clenched teeth. 'Whatever it was, it must be worth a very great deal and we are going to find it.'

'But how?'

'Men who can tip gold coins out like that don't just disappear,' she said in the singsong voice she reserved for idiots. 'They go somewhere else, and that is where we are going to go too.'

'But how?'

'Dolt!' she shouted and hit him with the lamp. 'We follow him and the boy. Don't forget the boy. He's a sly one. He knows more than he pretends to.'

The carriage carrying Dr Leiter and Mathias rolled on through the night. Mathias wanted to sleep, but he could not. When he closed his eyes, he kept seeing Gustav's face washed clean of its paint. If he managed to shut that out, he saw instead Gustav in the flickering torchlight and shadow, falling from the stage over and over again.

Then there was something else too. Though the leather blinds of the carriage were drawn, Mathias knew where they were. They were on the road that ran away from the town and through the thick forest. The same road that he had come down before in the circus cart. Even if it's dark and you cannot see a forest, you can hear when you are in one. You can. A forest sounds like no other thing anywhere. It buries sound like a blanket of fallen snow does, but it smells quite different. Even if you cannot see it, you can hear it. Even if you cannot hear it, you can smell the leaf mould and the damp earth.

So Mathias didn't need to see the forest to know where they were. He could hear the dead sound of it all around them. And he could hear something else as well.

He could hear wolves.

They had been following the carriage for a while now. He was certain of it. Sometimes there would be a bark like that of a dog, far away, then another one in answer, closer. If he listened carefully, he thought that he could hear them too – the sound of their running feet in the brush and bracken, keeping

pace with the carriage.

There was a small night lamp in the carriage. It was turned down as low as it could go – barely a glimmer. By that single worm of light Mathias could see that Leiter had his eyes shut. His head was jogging, keeping time to the motion of the carriage, as though he were asleep. Mathias didn't know whether he really was asleep or not. If he was, Mathias didn't want to wake him. But if he didn't, what might happen then? Finally he couldn't bear it any more. He tugged hard at Leiter's sleeve. Leiter's eyes opened instantly.

'There are wolves,' Mathias said.

Leiter closed his eyes again. 'It does not matter,'

he said.

'We have to build a fire.'

'We do not need a fire.'

Mathias had to make him understand. 'But they will kill the horses,' he said.

'They will not kill the horses,' said Leiter quietly, his eyes still shut. 'Valter will see to that.' He rapped on the roof again.

The carriage began to slow. Then it stopped. There was a bark from the forest to their left, answered by another, nearer, but from the other side. Then another. The wolves were all about them. The carriage rocked on its springs as if someone were climbing down, and all at once there was a confusion of noise, of the wolves seizing hold of something to tear it apart, each fighting for the chance to sink its teeth in. Mathias pressed his hands over his ears, but he still heard what happened next: the yelping of an animal in terrible pain, the noise cut short as though the life had been ripped out of whatever had made it. Then the same noise again, and suddenly all about the carriage, like a wind through the bracken, there was a rushing of wolves yelping and baying like curs chased with a whip. Then silence. Utter, incomprehensible silence.

Mathias turned his head one way then the other, listening. But there was no sound. The travelling box at the back of the carriage was opened and he heard what seemed like a long length of chain being drawn out. There were other sounds too. Of the chain being handled, of something being fastened to the axle of the carriage. Then the carriage rocked on its springs again as the driver climbed back into the seat. There was the smallest of jolts and the carriage began to move. In the far distance came one long mournful howl, then silence.

'You can sleep,' said Leiter. He leaned forward and snuffed out the light with his fingers. 'They will not bother us again.'

Mathias sat wide-eyed in the darkness. He didn't know what it was that had followed him in the shadows or what had climbed down from the carriage in the dark, but he was certain it was one and the same, and he knew in his bones that it was something to be very frightened of.

It even had a name.

Valter.

He couldn't remember going to sleep. He opened his eyes and it was bright daylight. The carriage was empty, the door open. He could hear the sound of hens scratching on the ground. Somewhere nearby a cock crowed and beat its wings. A girl was peering round the open door. It was she who'd woken him. She pushed at his boot and then snatched her hand back as though she were frightened he might bite her.

'Are you the boy?' she said. 'You've got to come. He's waiting.'

Muddled with sleep, Mathias stepped down from the carriage. He had to screw his eyes up against the brightness. They had stopped in a dirt road outside a small inn. Hens were pecking at the ground between the wheels. A small group of people stood staring at him and the carriage. There was frost in the air. In the daylight the horses seemed even bigger than they had looked in the night. Huge and black. The carriage was black too, like ink. But the people were looking at something else as well. Mathias turned and gasped.

Behind the carriage, fastened to it by a chain around their necks, were the bodies of two of the largest wolves Mathias had ever seen. Each was the size of a pony. They were stone dead, throats torn out, their eyes bulging with the terror of their deaths.

The people stepped back and made way for him as he walked towards the door. The girl went in front of him. She kept her distance, looking over her shoulder to make sure that he was following.

Inside, the inn was dark. It smelled of last night's wood smoke, and beer and spiced sausage. A man was sweeping the floor but he stopped working to watch Mathias follow the girl up the wooden staircase.

She was about Mathias's age, perhaps a little older. She wore a work apron over a rough skirt and blouse. She had deep auburn red hair tied tight at the back; it stuck out from beneath a padded leather cap. When they got to the top of the stairs, he followed her along a narrow corridor with windows that looked down onto the stable yard. At the end was a wooden door. She stood to one side.

'You knock,' she said in a quick, sharp voice, and he realized that she was frightened of knocking on the door. But he was frightened as well.

'What's your name?' he said.

She glanced at the door as though not wanting to be heard, not wanting to be part of this, whatever it was.

'Please?' he said.

5
Marguerite

Katta watched the cold, pale-faced boy go into the room and the door close behind him. It did not seem right. The tall man with the moon face and the silver-topped cane had scared her. The boy was nothing to do with him. She knew that as clearly as if she had been told it. But there he was, and there she was bringing him up the stairs and leading him to the room.

You know that some things are wrong even without breathing. It's wrong to tell a lie, but everyone does – sometimes. It's wrong to take a thing that isn't yours, or to hurt someone for the fun of doing it. But there are other things too, even bigger. Things that are so wrong that just the thought of them makes you shrink up inside and take a deep breath. That's how Katta felt as she watched the door close. Instinctively she almost reached out to catch hold of Mathias's coat to stop him going through, but she didn't, and then it was too late. The door had shut.

She took a step forward and very carefully put her ear to the wood. She could hear the man's voice, but she couldn't make out what it said. Someone began bawling for her from far downstairs. She tried hard to ignore them, to listen to what was happening in the room. But the downstairs voice grew more insistent – angry. She stepped back from the door, not knowing what to do. Then she took her skirt in her hands and ran down the corridor. But even so, she had to stop, just once, and look back. She couldn't help thinking of the pale boy and the expression on his face. But she was being shouted for, and there was nothing she could do about it anyway.

Inside the room there was a large bed with heavy, dark curtains about it. There was a chest, a wardrobe and a long table. The morning light fell through the small leaded panes of glass in the window and onto the table. All Gustav's things had been spread out on it. Dr Leiter sat at the table. He had taken off his coat and, with a bowl of water before him and a cut-throat razor in his hand, he was shaving. There were the remains of his breakfast upon a plate.

Mathias took all this in with one quick glance, then the door shut behind him and he turned to see who had closed it. Just for an instant he thought it was a child like him, or like the girl who had shown him to the room. But that impression lasted for only the most fleeting of moments because it was not a child at all. It was a man. He was not much taller than Mathias, heavy set, squashed like a tight barrel.

He wore a thick double-breasted overcoat that was fastened high under his chin. His hair was like dirty wire. It hung over the edge of the collar. Despite himself, Mathias gasped. The small man's face was misshapen, as though it had been quarter twisted when he was made. He looked back at Mathias, cocked his head mockingly to one side and smiled. It was a smile full of malice.

'Come in, boy,' said Leiter.

Mathias stepped forward. Behind him the small, barrel-chested man leaned his back against the door, then, in the same instant, quick as a cat, he turned and cocked his head as though he had heard something outside. Carefully he put his ear to the door. What he had heard was the very moment when Katta had put her head to the other side. She hadn't made a sound – I am afraid to say that she was very good at listening at doors. People who work in inns very often are. But for all her silence, that small man had heard her. Slowly he began to reach up for the door latch, but then a voice called from downstairs, then called again, and there was a sound of running footsteps receding down the corridor. They stopped once, but then went on again. Then there was no noise.

Leiter had seen it all. 'Has our little listener gone?' he said quietly.

The small man nodded and leaned his back against the door again.

Mathias did not like the idea of him standing there – as much a barrier to someone coming in as to him getting out. It gave him an uncomfortable feeling down the back of his neck. It was the same feeling as the night before, when he had realized that there was something following him in the dark.

'Are these all your grandfather's things?' asked Leiter. 'Come,' he said, beckoning to him. 'Take a good look at them.'

Mathias stepped slowly forward, not sure what it was he was supposed to say.

They were all there. The hollow spheres that Gustav had made glow and float, before sending them out over the heads of the crowd. All his tricks and illusions. His clothes. It all looked lifeless and empty without him. Every single thing on the table had been pulled apart or turned inside out.

'There is nothing missing?' asked Leiter.

'No,' said Mathias.

'Are you sure? Look again,' Leiter said.

Mathias shook his head. 'It's all there,' he said.

Leiter shaved the last of the soap from his face. Mathias could hear the hard bristles against the edge of the razor. Then Leiter patted his skin dry with a towel. Mathias stood waiting with his hands in his pockets, the small roll of paper held tightly in one fist. He had no doubt about it at all: this was what Leiter was looking for. He felt certain too that, if he once let that show upon his face, Leiter would see it. He tried hard to think of nothing at all.

'Your grandfather,' said Leiter. 'Did he ever give you anything to look after for him. Or tell you something very special or secret that you had to remember?'

'No,' said Mathias.

'No little keepsake or letter?'

Mathias shook his head dumbly.

'Perhaps we should just see,' said Leiter.

He reached down to the floor beside him and lifted a small, battered, green leather box onto the table. It was not very big, like a shoe box, about a foot high. He took a key from his pocket and opened it. The front folded out in two hinged doors. Inside, snug in the rich blue velvet lining, was a doll. She wore a fine court dress with the smallest flowers and birds woven into it.

'This is Marguerite,' said Leiter, carefully lifting the doll onto the table.

Mathias found himself leaning forward. The doll was quite perfect, like a very small, living person but with her eyes shut, as though fast asleep. He had never seen a toy like it before.

'Marguerite always travels with me,' said Leiter. 'I find her so helpful if people try to lie to me. You see, she can do something wholly remarkable.' He looked steadily at Mathias with his hard dark eyes. 'She can tell the difference between the truth and a lie. It is extraordinary. But she is never wrong. I will show you.'

Leiter took from the box two small cards, a blue one and a red one. He laid them on the tabletop in front of the doll, then, with his fingernail, tapped on the table in front of her. For a moment she did not move, then, to Mathias's astonishment, as though she had been deep in other thoughts, she shook her head daintily and looked up at Leiter.

'Marguerite,' he said, and the little doll gave a curtsey and looked intently at him with her hands folded across her lap.

'This boy is called Ludovic.' He pointed to Mathias and the doll turned her head to look. Then she bent forward and very lightly laid her hand on the red card. Her face showed no expression as she did so.

'Ah,' said Leiter. 'Marguerite knows that is not true. Tell her your real name, boy.'

'Mathias.'

Marguerite bent forward and this time touched the blue card.

'You see,' said Leiter. 'Marguerite can hear what is true. The two things must sound very different to her, and she can tell. It matters not how you try to say it. She can always tell.'

He looked at Mathias and suddenly Mathias understood what was about to happen. Leiter was going to ask him the questions again, only this time the doll would hear too.

'Did Gustav ever tell you a secret?' he said.

Mathias hesitated. 'No,' he said.

He watched wide-eyed as Marguerite bent forward, but unhesitatingly she touched the blue card. As she did so, Mathias realized that she was right. Gustav had never told him the secret. He had only ever said that he knew one and that was something quite different. Mathias hadn't told a lie.

Leiter sat back in his chair and thought for a

moment. 'Then did he give you anything to look after for him?' he said.

This is going to be easy, thought Mathias. Because he didn't give the paper to me.

'No,' he said, this time more confidently.

Again Marguerite touched the blue card.

'Did you ever hear or see him tell anyone anything secret?'

Again when Mathias answered, the doll touched the blue card. How did she do it? he thought. But it didn't matter because Leiter couldn't ask him anything else, or so it seemed to Mathias.

But he was wrong.

Leiter had been about to put the doll back into its box when it seemed that, almost as an afterthought, he said, 'Have you ever taken anything that belonged to your grandfather?'

Mathias felt the blood drain from his face. His mouth went suddenly dry. 'What like?' he said, but his voice was unsteady.

Leiter heard it and looked up at him with dangerous attention. 'Just answer the question,' he said slowly.

Mathias swallowed. 'No,' he said.

The word came out as little more than a whisper,

but it was loud enough for Marguerite to hear. She bent slowly forward and touched the red card.

'Ahh,' said Leiter in a voice like honey. 'A liar and a thief. Tut tut. I wonder what it was you took. Do you still have it, boy?'

Mathias could feel the hard fold of paper in his fist. 'No,' he said.

Marguerite bent down and touched the red card.

'Well,' breathed Leiter. 'You had better show it to me.'

Mathias looked from Leiter to the door as though he might try to run, but the small man stood in his way. 'But the doll's wrong,' he stammered.

Leiter shook his head. 'Marguerite is never wrong,' he said.

Seemingly unmoved, the little doll folded her hands neatly across her lap. Then she parted her pretty lips and smiled, but all her teeth were pointed, like a row of small, sharp needles.

'You had better give it to me,' said Leiter, and he held out his hand, 'or Valter will have to take it from you, and you must believe me when I tell you that you really would not want him to do that.'

Mathias looked at the small man. He had already guessed who it had to be. Valter's eyes had taken on a cold, unfocused glaze. It was the expression you would see on an executioner's face if you looked at it at the very moment he let the trapdoor drop.

'Give it to me,' said Dr Leiter.

Katta knew whose voice it was – it was the cook's. The kitchen was at the back of the inn. It had low dark ceilings from which hens and geese, still in their feathers, hung on hooks in the rafters, ready for the pot. Even this early in the day the place was full of steam and smoke, thick with the smell of cut vegetables and roasting meat. The cook should have been a large, smiling, fat woman with red forearms like hams, and cheeks like apples, but she wasn't. She was a slattern who spat on the fruit to clean it. Katta had seen her lift the meat from plates already on their way to table and, just for the spite of it, lick it and put it back, laughing. Katta hated her. Once she had made Katta, without a cloth for her hand, lift a full pot that had been standing above the fire, just because Katta had been too slow pulling the feathers from a goose. She still had the marks of the burn on her fingers.

A tray of breakfast had been made ready to carry. On it was a pot of scalding coffee, sliced meats, butter and bread.

'Take it upstairs,' said the cook, wiping her hands upon her dirty apron. 'The old man, at the end above the arch.'

Katta had done as she was told. She carried the tray back up the stairs, but when she came to the top, she stopped. One way led to the old man's room – she knew which one the cook had meant: he'd been there for three days already and always had his breakfast this way; the other led back to the room where she had left the boy. Not entirely certain in her own mind why, she turned and went that way instead. It was some unthought thing, to do with wanting to be sure that he was safe. Bad things can happen in closed rooms – she had learned that to her cost. But this wasn't a conscious thought at all. It was just something she found she was doing. She even knew what she was going to say – that she had brought the breakfast to the wrong room. She would see that the boy was all right, and she would come away.

But it didn't happen like that. What happened was this.

She knocked on the door and pushed it open with the tray, all in one practised movement. The tall, moon-faced man was standing in his black silk waist-coat and white shirt sleeves with his back to her. The short coachman – she had seen him only once – had the boy gripped by the neck and was shaking him like a rat out of the open window. The boy was kicking and gasping for breath. His face was blue.

All in the same moment that she took the sight in, the man heard the sound of the door opening behind him and spun round. Katta screamed and dropped the tray with a crash. The coachman turned his face towards her and, quite deliberately, opened his hand. The boy made one wild grab at the window frame, missed it, and dropped from sight like a stone.

6

The Pile of Barrels

Mathias felt quiet and strangely warm, as though he were wrapped in the blankets of a deep, soft feather bed. He could feel the weight of them pressing down upon his chest, holding him so that he couldn't move at all. Dimly he understood that something had happened to him, but he didn't know what. Didn't know, until it started to hurt. Then he opened his eyes and the world was suddenly cold and sharp and hard – and he couldn't breathe at all. He was lying flat on his back on the frosted ground, looking up at the blue morning sky and an open window high above him. He saw a head lean out, then disappear back inside. In that instant, like dropped picture cards, he remembered everything.

Dr Leiter. The doll. The dwarf.

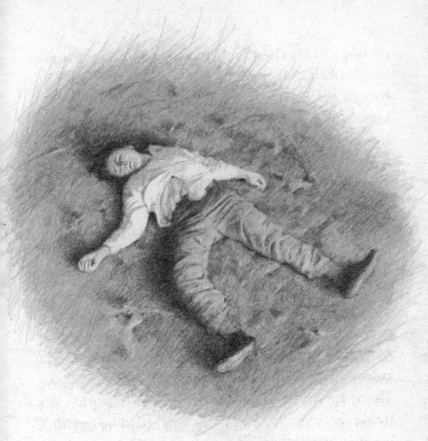

He knew he had to get up and run, but he couldn't move. Every last atom of breath had slammed from him as he hit the ground. Now his lungs were crying out for air, but his chest simply would not work. All he could manage was small, teaspoon sips of breath. He pulled himself onto his side and began to crawl. He could feel bone grating on bone in his chest and knew that something there had broken. But crawling was too slow. He knew he had to get up and run. He lifted himself onto his knees, and cried out in pain as the ends of his snapped ribs ground one against another. Then, bent double and stumbling, he tried to find somewhere to hide. If they caught him, it was very simple – they were going to kill him.

Giddy with pain, he looked around at the swimming world and tried to make sense of it. He had been dropped from a window at the back of the inn. It was a wonder the fall hadn't killed him outright. It was only the filth and dirty straw on the ground that had saved him. There was an old barn, its door hanging open. He knew it would be the first place they looked. Behind it though was rough ground and then the edge of the forest. He could see the deep cover of trees and bracken. If he could only reach the trees. He tried to straighten up and run but his chest hurt too much. He could hear noises from the inn – people shouting. He wrapped his arms around himself and, squeezing his chest as tightly as he dared, stumbled towards the trees.

He had nearly passed the open door of the old barn when a hand reached out from it, caught hold of his coat and snatched him in. Blindly he lashed out, felt his fist in a face, but whoever it was pulled him down and he hadn't the strength to stop them. He cried out, and a hand went tight over his mouth to silence him. He bit it as hard as he could, heard the person whimper, but the hand pressed tighter still.

'Sssh!'

In the half-light a face pressed close to his.

'Sssh!' the voice said again.

Then he saw who it was. It was the girl, Katta.

When Katta dropped the tray, Leiter and Valter had both stared at her for a moment. Then Leiter spun on his heels and leaped for the door, Valter close behind him.

'Thief!' Leiter shouted, and they were out of the room and down the hall, Leiter still shouting at the top of his voice. 'Thief! Stop him!'

But Katta knew that wasn't what she'd seen happening.

She took one quick look from the open window – it was her head that Mathias had seen: the boy was lying motionless on the ground and she thought that he must be dead. But then he moved. She didn't stop to think. The two men had gone the wrong way if they were going to get behind the inn before she did. She knew a much quicker way than that. She ran from the room, along the gallery and down the back stairs that led straight to the stable yard. Holding her skirts up, she tore across the yard and through a gap little wider than she was. As she squeezed through the other end, she could see the boy on his feet, stumbling towards the trees. She felt a wave of relief that he could stand. But she could hear more voices now. They were coming. He had no chance at all of reaching the wood. But if she could get to the old barn before him . . .

Still not thinking why she was doing it, she ran back the way she'd come, ducked through a hole in the barn wall and, pushing her way in the dark past the piled rubbish of barrels and timber, reached the doorway only seconds before Mathias did. There was just enough time to snatch hold of him and pull him down into the shadows. She barely felt him hit her or bite her hand.

'Sssh!' she hissed, and pushed her face close to his so that he could see who it was. Her heart was pounding. 'Sssh!'

She saw his eyes widen in startled recognition and

took her hand from his mouth. She tried to pull him up by his arm. He moaned and she realized that he must be hurt, but there was no time for kindness. With both hands she caught hold of his collar and dragged him inside. He could hear voices, louder now, as men came round the back of the inn. They stopped momentarily beneath the window where he had fallen. It was only an instant before they saw the barn and realized that he was probably there.

Katta pulled him over the floor. The tar-soaked planks scraped against his face. He could feel her, one-handed, pulling at something that creaked, then moved. There was a draught of cold, damp air around him. She pulled him down into it as the men burst into the old building. Mathias fell heavily against soft earth. He reached out to steady himself, but his fingers found only empty air. There was a quiet thump, as though something had closed above them, and then damp, dark quiet. He could hear the sound of the girl breathing. She pressed close against him and laid a finger across his lips.

'Sssh,' she whispered. He found himself, with stupid clarity, wondering if it were the only sound that she could make.

He could hear other things now, the noises of the

search – voices, things being dragged about – but they were muffled, as though all that was happening in another place. Then the sounds grew suddenly close and he felt the girl tighten against him. The pain in his chest made him whimper, but he bit it back. Leiter would find him now. He could still feel Valter's hand around his throat, see the ground far below his dangling feet. He wanted to shout out for somebody to come and help him, but the girl had her hand over his mouth again as though she'd guessed what he might do.

In the barn the men from the inn, the groom and stable lads had searched everywhere. Peered into every place. Now they had lost interest. They looked at Leiter.

'He's not here, sir,' they said.

Leiter, an unasked question on his face, turned to Valter. The dwarf had taken no part in any of it. He stood indifferently in the middle of the floor, collar up, hands stuffed deep into the pockets of his thick coat. He returned Leiter's look and gave an almost imperceptible nod of his head, barely moving it at all. But Leiter knew exactly what it meant.

'Well,' Leiter said, 'it seems the young wretch has got away. It was not too much he took, I suppose.'

He put his hand into his pocket and drew out a few meagre coins. 'This is for your trouble,' he said, and tossed them to the men to share out amongst themselves.

As an insult it was well calculated. They'd expected more reward for their help than a few paltry coins. What little interest they had left in Leiter evaporated in an instant. One of them contemptuously spat on the coin he'd been given, but he still took it. They trailed from the barn, one or two looking back sourly. Leiter waited until they were out of sight and then turned to Valter. The dwarf still hadn't moved.

'He is hiding here?' said Leiter.

Valter nodded.

Leiter smiled. 'Then you had better find him,' he said.

Valter got down onto his hands and knees, like a large dog. He bent forward and smelled the ground, then put his head to one side and listened. He did this several times, all the while moving closer to where a pile of barrels stood against one wall of the barn. Finally he got up and looked at Leiter.

'Here?' said Leiter.

Valter nodded. He began to move the heavy

barrels away, rolling each one as easily as if it had been made of paper, until there was nothing left but one barrel and the bare floor.

'Are you sure?' said Leiter.

Valter gripped the barrel. But it didn't move as the others had done. He looked at it as though puzzled. Then he pushed it. With a click, it tipped backwards. Where it had stood was an open hatchway, and a darkness from which a draught of cold, damp air came. It was the place where Mathias and Katta had hidden.

Only now it was empty.

7

Through the Dark

Katta had not been able to make Mathias understand just what it was they had to do. She hadn't dared speak above a whisper, and though she kept tugging at his coat, she couldn't get him to move. He slumped in the dark, his breath coming in short, painful gasps. It was pitch dark all about them. So dark that he couldn't see what she already knew – that they were at the opening of a low tunnel, not quite high enough for a man to stand fully upright in. It ran beneath the barn and curved away into the forest. At its other end there was a track. Not a track that was meant to be noticed, but it was there all right. A lot of people came and went from that inn. A lot of things too, not all of them meant to be seen – small barrels and rolls of fine cloth – things that had never seen an excise man or paid the tax due.

Things that took the back roads and were gone the next day. That's what the tunnel was for. That was what the inn was really about, and anyone who interfered or asked too many questions just wasn't seen again.

Katta had found the tunnel quite by accident one wet day, climbing amongst the barrels in the old barn. She had even been down it, just once. It had scared her so. The roots of the trees trailing through the earth roof, the smell of the damp, the small showers of soil falling on her as she passed beneath. She'd been terrified that at any moment the roof might come down on her in one suffocating collapse, burying her deeper than any grave. She'd gone just as far as she could dimly see, then her nerve had given out and she'd scrambled back to the opening, her heart pounding and her skin wet with fear.

But it was the first thing that came to her when she'd seen Mathias trying to reach the trees – that she could hide him in the tunnel. It was only as she closed the hatch above their heads and felt the suddenly irresistible weight of the barrel drop back down with that ominous thump that she realized she couldn't open it again. She hadn't needed to close it the time before – she'd found it open and left it that way. Perhaps Mathias could have helped her push it, but he was barely able to stand. She could feel the cold damp air against her face and instantly knew what they would have to do. That air had to be coming from somewhere. With the hatch shut there was nothing for it but to go down into the dark until they came to the other end of the tunnel and hope that there was a way out. It was as this was running through her mind and she was trying in whispered words to make Mathias understand that she heard the sound of the barrels, one by one, being slowly and purposefully cleared from the floor above them. There was no time left. She grabbed Mathias by his coat and, not caring about the noise he made, shook him until she got him to stand up; then, taking hold of his arm, she pulled him after her into the dark.

Valter did not make a noise as he dropped through the hatchway into the dark space beneath it. Leiter stooped above him but made no effort to climb down. He had found a lamp and lit it.

'It will be something small enough for him to have hidden,' he said. 'Find it, do you understand? Pull each one of his teeth from his head if you have to, but find it and bring it back to me.'

He handed Valter the lamp. Valter took it, grinned and, like a cat, was gone.

The tunnel curved and wound. About halfway along it had been dug wider to make a place in which things could be stacked. Katta, with one hand outstretched, the other dragging Mathias behind her, had groped her way along the wall until, not knowing it, she had come to that place. She couldn't see a thing in the blackness, but there was a different smell in the damp air – sweet, of tarred wood and apples. It was as she stopped and tried to understand, to catch her breath and listen, that she realized that where a moment before it had seemed quite dark, now she could see the palest glimmer of light. It was just enough to make out dim shapes. For an instant she felt a wave of relief. She thought that they must have arrived close enough to the other end of the tunnel for the daylight to reach in. But then she went quite cold inside. The edge of the light was moving along the wall. It wasn't daylight at all. There was someone with a lamp coming down the tunnel behind them.

*

Valter didn't have to rush. This was the kind of game he liked best. The kind where people thought they could hide from him. Sometimes he liked to let them think that he couldn't find them. He'd pretend just long enough so they believed that they were really safe. Then he could watch their faces as all hope vanished, and they understood not just that there was nowhere they could hide from him, but that he had known where they were all the time.

That was when Valter's fun really began.

There was something else too. Something that Valter knew which Leiter didn't. As he dropped down through the floor, he had breathed in. Yes. He was right. The boy was here – he could smell him. But he could smell something else too, and for a moment he was puzzled. He could smell almond paste and cooking, sweeping and hard work. It was a smell he could not place at once but vaguely recognized. Then it came to him. It was the smell of the serving girl. The one who had listened at the door. For an instant he hesitated. Should he tell Leiter? But Leiter didn't need to know and it would make for so much more fun, there being two of them to play with.

He held the lamp out in front of him, drew a long,

sharp knife from beneath his coat and began to walk slowly down the tunnel.

Katta looked desperately about her. Mathias didn't understand what was happening at all. He had lumbered along behind her in the dark; now he stood still, swaying on his feet as though he might drop at any moment. She could run, but he couldn't. The light was growing stronger. She could clearly see what the shapes around her were now: barrels and boxes. Lengths of wrapped oilcloth, all tied and strapped ready for the pack ponies. It was all piled up against the walls. She had to decide – there was no more time: the lamp would come round the bend in the tunnel at any moment and they'd be seen. They had to run or hide.

There really was no choice.

They had to hide.

Valter came round the bend. In the lamplight he could see the stacked boxes, the barrels and the oilcloth, and he knew at once that was where they were. He stopped. He couldn't see them, but he didn't have to. He could breathe them in amongst the brandy and barrels, the smell of boy and the smell of girl, close by. He cocked his head a little to one side and listened. He could even hear the quick sound of their hearts beating. No. No one had ever managed to hide from Valter.

Through the narrowest crack between a pile of barrels, Katta watched the dwarf. He stood with his back to her, holding the lamp up as he searched amongst the boxes on the other side of the tunnel. She ducked down just before he turned and the light swept past the place where they hid. She heard him moving things about and held her breath. But he didn't find them. He walked on. She could hear the soft sound his coachman's boots made on the earth floor as he went by. The light of the lamp grew fainter and fainter as he moved away. Then it was dark again. She let her breath go in a long, quiet whisper of relief. But now he was between them and their way out. Maybe, she thought, he would reach the end and come back above ground through the wood. Either way they were safe for the moment. They would just have to wait a bit longer. She settled back, and it was at this moment that Valter's hand came slowly out of the dark and gripped her hair.

She screamed.

The dwarf had crept silently back in the darkness, the lamp and knife wrapped beneath his thick coat. Now he had Katta by her long hair, he drew the lamp out again so that he could look at her face as he pulled her from between the barrels. The boy was on the ground behind her. He hadn't moved even when she screamed, but he was looking up at Valter with wide-eyed terror.

This was going to be a good game.

Valter flung Katta away – it was the boy he wanted first; he could play with her later. She crashed hard into the heavy boxes, all the breath knocked from her. The boxes swayed and fell on her. Pulling the knife from his coat, the dwarf reached down and, in one quick movement, passed it straight through Mathias's shoulder.

'Where is it?' he said.

He pushed the knife through again. There was nowhere for Mathias to go. The dwarf dragged him out over the top of the barrels, threw him roughly to the ground, then sat astride him with the knife sideways between his teeth and his thumbs pressed hard into Mathias's eyes.

'Where is it?'

Katta's head was ringing. She could see the dwarf

on Mathias. She looked about for something she could use to hit him with. There was only the oil lamp. The dwarf had put it down on the ground beside him. She got unsteadily to her feet, picked it up and swung it as hard as she could. It hit Valter on the back of the head with a dull crack. The glass shattered, and instantly he was on fire. The oil from the lamp was thick in his hair; it soaked into his coat. He leaped up wildly, beating at the flames with his hands, but he was like a burning torch. The more he beat at them, the more the flames caught hold, until he was all fire. Screaming, he blundered blindly into

8
The Stranger on the Horse

Katta saw the roof fall. It seemed to happen so slowly, though it couldn't have been like that. Streams of earth, like sheets of cloth, fell on the burning dwarf; then it all came down in one rush, burying him and the flames beneath tons of soil. The tunnel plunged into an instant darkness that one moment was full of noise – of earth and splintering wood – and the next was suddenly silent like a grave. The whole roof above where the dwarf had been had come down on him. Katta stood absolutely still in the dark, holding her breath, not daring to move so much as a muscle, lest the rest of the roof come down on her. She could hear the timbers above her head creaking and groaning. Very slowly, she bent down and put her hands under Mathias's shoulders. The boy didn't move; didn't make any sound at all. She didn't know if he was alive or dead. Whimpering with the terror of doing it so slowly – so slowly – she dragged him away, backwards through the dark, while the tunnel roof creaked and groaned, and it only needed for her to brush against the walls to bring it all down and bury them too.

But she managed it. She turned a bend and there was a weak, grey light all around her that had nothing to do with any lamp. She looked backwards over her shoulder and could see a square of daylight. She didn't feel so frightened now that she could see it, but she didn't dare go any faster. She made herself concentrate on Mathias's face. It was ashen, but now there was enough light to see by, she was sure that he was still alive. She wondered what on earth he had done that could have made this happen? What was it that the dwarf had wanted?

Branches had been piled across the opening of the tunnel to hide it. She pushed them away, then dragged Mathias out through the litter of fallen leaves into the cold daylight. She stood and caught her breath. The wood was thick with frost and silence. She knelt down beside Mathias, scared of what she would find. Very carefully she undid the buttons of his coat. She could see the two slits in his shirt where Valter's knife had gone clean through. The shirt was sodden with dark blood. She tore at the hem of her skirt to make a bandage, but even as she did so, something very hard and cold was pressed firmly into the back of her neck. She felt, as much as heard, the click as the hammer of the pistol was pulled back.

Her shoulders dropped. They must have been waiting there all the time. It was so unfair. Her eyes filled with tears.

She was pulled to her feet and turned round, but it wasn't Leiter that Katta saw, or anyone else from the inn. There were four men standing before her. A fifth – a tall man – sat astride a big bay horse. His coat and boots were soiled with mud as though he had ridden a long way. The collar of his coat was turned up against the cold, but not enough to hide the scarf of finest Spanish lace that was wound around his neck.

'And what have we here?' he said.

Katta was still holding the strip of cloth she had torn from her skirt. She wiped her wet eyes with the back of her hand.

'Please,' she said. 'He's hurt.'

The man's eyes went slowly from her to Mathias

and back again. 'What were you doing in there?'

It was as though he hadn't heard.

Then she realized who these people must be. The barrels and the oilcloth bags in the tunnel, all the things stacked and waiting – they were waiting to be collected. These must be the men. With that thought, she knew that there was no hope. Everyone knew what these men did to people who interfered, who found out what they shouldn't know. She had to think quickly. She had to make them believe that she hadn't seen anything.

'We was playing,' she said. 'It's a cave in there, but you can't go in very far 'cos the roof's all down.' She pointed to Mathias. 'He got hurt on some sharp stuff. I don't know what. It's all dark in there.'

The man's face became a frown. He turned to one of the other men. 'Go and see,' he said.

There were packhorses standing quietly nearby. Katta hadn't seen them until then. One of the men fetched a lamp from a saddlebag, then, bending over it, lit it from the flint in his pistol and disappeared into the tunnel.

Katta could feel the tall man looking at her, but she didn't want to look back. Instead she stared around, up into the bare trees, the sky above them, anywhere else but at him.

The lamp man came back. 'It's all down,' he said. 'Just before halfway.'

'Any way through?' said the man on the horse.

The other shook his head. 'No. It's solid.'

Despite herself, Katta couldn't help but look at the man on the horse, trying to see what he would do next. For a few moments he didn't speak. She could see him turning it all over in his mind.

'We'll try the other way,' he said.

The men nodded and went back towards the horses.

Katta bit her lip. He had believed her. She could feel hope rising inside her. He was going to leave them there.

'Where are you from?' the tall man asked.

'Cottage in the wood,' she said, jerking her head. That might have been enough, but she wanted to make it sound convincing, so she said. 'It's just over there.'

As soon as she pointed, she knew she had made a mistake. He must know these woods far better than she did. He'd been about to turn his horse away, but when she said that, he reined it in again and stopped.

'Where?' he said.

She pointed again, trying not to seem as vague as she had the first time. He gave a sharp whistle and the other men stopped too.

'There's no cottage out that way,' he said. 'Not for a long mile.'

'It's very small,' she said, but she knew it was too late. He'd already stopped believing her.

He got down from his horse and went over to where Mathias lay on the ground. He pulled open the coat and saw the blood-soaked shirt. 'Anyone know who she is?' he said.

The men came back. They all looked at Katta.

'She's the girl from the inn,' said one hesitantly. 'The one who bangs her head about.'

They had all gathered round her now.

'That's a blade did that,' the tall man said to her. 'What were you doing in there?'

This time there was menace in his voice. She knew she would have to watch each word.

'Hiding,' she said. 'They wanted the boy.'

'Who did? Tahlmann?'

It was the name of the innkeeper.

'No. Someone else. I hid him from them.'

The man's face gave nothing away. 'But you came

through the tunnel?' he said.

'No,' she lied. 'We just found it here.'

'Why did they want the boy?'

'I don't know. They dropped him out of a window.'

The tall man looked at her for a moment, then laughed out loud. 'What a lot of lies you can tell,' he said.

'But it's true,' she said. 'The dwarf dropped him out of the window. He chased us, but the roof came down on him.'

And she realized that she had done it again.

'But you didn't come through the tunnel, did you?' said the man. 'You found this end. That's what you said. The tunnel was already down.'

She opened her mouth, but no words would come. The man turned away from her.

'Pick up the boy,' he said to the others. 'Put him on my horse.'

He got back onto the big animal and they handed Mathias up, set him in the saddle in front of the tall man.

'You walk,' he said to Katta. 'If you try to run, I'll finish the boy. Do you understand?'

She looked up at him and nodded.

'Cover it up,' he said to the others. 'There's no digging it out now.'

The men put back the branches that Katta had moved, and swept leaves across the place. You wouldn't have known it was there. Then, following the man on the big horse, they led the ponies back along the track through the wood to the road. After a few words, they parted company. The men and the ponies went one way and the tall man, with Mathias lolling in the saddle and Katta walking beside his horse, went the other – back into the wood.

Beneath the tons of fallen earth, something began to move. At first he could only move his fingertips; he had to work them until they made a small space. Then he was able to move his whole hand. In the buried darkness, Valter began to dig his way free. There was nothing that could stop him.

One thought filled his vicious, empty heart as he clawed his way up through the earth, and that was to find the boy and the girl who had burned him and buried him and left him for dead. Find them, and then what a game they would have.

It took him several hours. It was long after nightfall before he pulled himself out of the ground and

spat the last of the earth from his mouth. He stood
amongst the trees in the wood, with the cold frosted
stars above him, and let out one long, murderous
cry. Then, with eyes sharper than any cat's, he
started searching in the wood for the opening of the
tunnel. That took him time as well, but he did not
rush. Just before dawn he found it below a grass
bank, branches pulled across. He knelt down and
breathed in. He could smell Mathias's blood
amongst the leaves. The smell of Katta where she

had knelt beside him. There were other smells too: of men – he could make out five – and horses, lots of horses. He listened until he was quite certain they weren't still close by. When he was satisfied that there was no sound to hear, he began to follow one scent – the scent of a girl walking beside a horse. It went step by step back along the hidden track through the wood to the road. In the darkness he smiled to himself. This was the best start for a game – when they thought themselves already safe.

9

The Burners

Katta walked beside the horse. The carpet of leaves on the ground was rimed with frost. She had no coat. She folded her arms about her, trying to keep warm, but the cold went straight through. Her feet were frozen. She didn't know where she was being taken, but she could guess only too easily how it would all end, when there was no one about to hear her scream or see what was done. That's how it would be.

But the horse walked on, and with each step Katta became more uncertain. She had seen enough dips and hollows – the quiet places where it could be done. Each time she steeled herself for the moment when the tall man would rein in the horse and get down. But he had ridden past them all. The morning had worn on and still they hadn't stopped.

There had to be an explanation, and she had to work out what it was.

When she thought that she had, she stopped walking. 'I'm not going any further,' she said.

But the horse carried on.

'I'm not going any further!' she shouted.

The man reined in and looked back at her but she stood her ground.

'You're not going to kill him, are you? 'Cos you want to know what they wanted, don't you? He might be worth something. That's it, isn't it?'

He walked the horse back towards her. Still holding Mathias with one hand, with the other hand he pulled a pistol from a leather fold on the saddle, cocked it and levelled it at Katta's head. 'Maybe I should just shoot you,' he said.

She could feel herself shaking, and this time it wasn't from the cold. But she'd worked that out too. She only hoped that she was right because it was too late now if she wasn't.

'You're not going to do that, neither. Are you?'

'Am I not?'

'No,' she said. ''Cos you'd have done it already if you was.'

A look of mild amusement passed across his face.

'But you weren't being a trouble before,' he said.

'Then you'd better get it over and done with,' she answered. ''Cos I can be a lot more trouble than this.'

She stood still, waiting for him to pull the trigger. It seemed like an age. She could see the dark, unwavering circle of the barrel in front of her face, the trees and the blue sky behind it. She wondered if they were the last things that she would see.

But he didn't pull the trigger. He put the pistol up and slid it back into its holster on the saddle. Then, reaching down, he took hold of her arm, pulled her up and set her behind him on the horse.

'Just don't think of being too much of a trouble quite yet,' he said. He clicked his tongue at the horse. 'Go on, Razor,' he said, and the horse shook its head and was away.

The man rode the horse on as though he wanted to make up for lost time. At one point they had to ford a river, but the big horse didn't hesitate. It stepped down through the cat ice at the water's edge and, blowing short, snorting breaths, half walked, half swam its way across the freezing water – the swirling cold bit into Katta's legs. Then the horse was up the other bank in huge, lunging strides. Katta had to hang onto the man's coat as they plunged back into the woods again. She almost forgot the cold. She'd seen lots of horses at the inn, even sat on a few, but never one as fine as this. She could imagine it riding down anyone foolish enough to stand in its way. It was huge, like a big wall of muscle and bone, and it just kept going.

They had ridden for at least another hour when Katta caught the smell of wood smoke in the cold air. First thin, then getting stronger. The man slowed the horse to a walk. Ahead, in a clearing, something was burning. She could see thick, blue-white smoke drifting like mist between the trees. The man leaned forward and slapped the horse's neck. It shook its head. Wherever it was that they were going, they had evidently arrived.

As the horse walked on, Katta looked about her. Stacks of felled wood were lying on the ground – split and heaped together. In several places large, turfed mounds leaked smoke. The clearing was thick with it. There were men working, their faces black, smeared with burned wood and ash. With iron spades they were patting and tending the turfed mounds, building new ones around stacked wood. There were small huts, the roofs thatched with

rough bracken, smoke leaking through them. Wherever she looked there was smoke. Her eyes stung with it. But she knew what this was. It was a Burners' camp. The people who felled the wood and smoked it through until it was nothing but sticks of charcoal. They'd stay in one place just long enough to make as much as they needed, then they'd move on, selling it by the sack load in the towns and villages as they went. They had their own language and ways. They didn't mix with the outside world and the outside world didn't mix with them. There was usually a lot of trouble when it did.

Several faces turned towards them. One of the men put down his spade and walked slowly towards them across the clearing. His face and clothes were grimed with charcoal, his eyes bloodshot. But he was smiling, his teeth white against the dirt of his face. He had a gold ring in each ear.

'Koenig!'

He said the name in friendly greeting, and Katta knew that this must be what the tall man was called. Then the Burner man saw Mathias, half wrapped in Koenig's coat, and, looking from the boy to Koenig, he reached up and with both hands carefully lifted Mathias down. Koenig slipped from the saddle and followed the man as he carried Mathias into one of the huts. Katta sat on the back of the big horse. Then she too swung her leg across and dropped to the ground. Some of the children who had been outside the huts stared at her. She stared back, then spat. She had once been in a fight with Burner children when they had passed the inn. It had been a long time ago, but she hadn't forgiven them for what they'd done. It was why she had to wear the padded hat.

It wasn't even her who had started it – it was the stableboys. They were always up for a fight. But she'd stood at the edge and watched it with glee, clapping her hands and yelling. It had got so bad that men had spilled out of the inn and pulled them all apart. Then one of the Burner boys had thrown a stone. A big stone, about the size of a goose egg. She'd seen him skulking at the back of the fight, too scared to get close. She saw him bend down and, scooping something up, throw it. She didn't see where it went – she lost the line of it above everyone else; then it hit her on the side of her head and the whole world shattered into little tiles of brightly coloured light. She found herself on her knees as though someone had put her there, but she didn't know how. Everywhere she turned, the world was made up of bright flickering colours. No one else had seen it happen. The fight was still being broken up; no one paid any attention to her. But suddenly she didn't feel well, and she didn't want to watch any more. Slowly, almost unaware of where she was, she had walked back through the door of the inn, the colours flickering in front of her eyes as she went. She could hear people talking, but their voices were deep and slow, as though she were hearing them through a wall. Someone gave her a tray to carry and it had dropped through her fingers. She had watched it floating slowly down to the ground like a falling feather. Then the ground came up and met her too.

and heavy, in her hand. At least, now, she had some thing that she could use if she had to, and there was no knowing whether she might need it before long.

She stopped in the doorway. For a moment she couldn't see a thing. Then her eyes grew accustomed to the gloom. It was dark and narrow inside the hut. Mathias had been laid on a rough, rug-covered bed – there was only one. There were pans and things she couldn't make out hanging from the roof above her. There was a woman too, her face weather-tanned and lined. Koenig and the man had already begun to unbutton Mathias's coat and pull his shirt over his head. He let out a moan and a hiss of breath as they sat him up to do it. The woman hushed him, then turned and said something to Katta in Burner. Katta shook her head, but then understood what the woman must have meant, and stepped to one side so that the light could come in.

With her fingertips, the woman carefully felt around the edges of the two knife wounds, trying to gauge how deep they were.

'And his chest,' Katta said. 'He's hurt his chest bad too.'

She felt suddenly uneasy, as though they might think that she had been responsible. 'They dropped him out of a window,' she said. 'He was holding his chest when I found him.'

She caught Koenig's eye, and remembered that he'd already called her a liar once. 'They did!' she said.

But Koenig looked away. She didn't know why she should be bothered about his opinion anyway. He was nothing but a thief.

The woman washed the blood away, then, making a pad from leaves, she spooned thick paste onto it from a clay pot and pressed it over the wounds. She took the shawl from her own shoulders and used it to bind the pad in place, tightly wrapping the thick cloth round and round Mathias's chest. Then she made him drink something that smelled sweet and earthy, and his head lolled almost at once and he closed his eyes.

She said something to Katta and pointed at the bed. By signs Katta understood that she had to stay beside Mathias, so she sat down and watched. The woman reached up and pulled down two dead rabbits that were hanging from a hook in the rafters above her head. Then she set herself on a stool in the doorway and, pulling a sharp knife from her belt, began to skin them. Koenig and the man had

116

already gone outside. Through the doorway Katta could see them standing and talking. Koenig was doing most of the talking; the other man listened. Once or twice he nodded, then looked back at the hut, and Katta knew that they were talking about her. She leaned back into the dark so that she could still watch them and not be seen herself. Then she had the thought that the woman had set herself in the doorway as much to stop her from going out as to skin the rabbits. She looked down at Mathias: he was deep in a drugged sleep. But they hadn't hurt him. For the moment he was safe. But she wasn't so sure about herself. She slipped the stone into the pocket of her apron and held onto it tightly.

Koenig finished talking to the man, who went back across the clearing. Koenig came towards the hut. He said something to the woman in the doorway that Katta couldn't understand, then leaned in and beckoned to Katta.

'Why can't they talk proper words like everyone else?' she said as she got up.

'I'd be careful what you say if I were you,' said Koenig. 'Some of them can.'

Katta looked quickly at the woman to see if she had understood what had been said. It's one thing to be rude about someone; it's quite another thing for them to understand it, especially when they're holding a knife. But the woman carried on skinning the rabbits and Katta guessed that she hadn't understood anything. It made her bold again.

'Then they should learn proper talk,' she said.

She followed Koenig to where a small fire burned in the clearing. He held out his hands to warm them. Now she had the chance to look at him properly, she saw that he was younger than she had thought. It must have been the way the men in the wood obeyed him that had made him seem older. The big horse hadn't been tethered. It was standing quietly nearby with its reins looped about its neck. Someone had piled some hay on the ground for it to eat.

'Your horse will walk off,' she said.

Koenig glanced over his shoulder. 'What, Razor?' he said.

The horse lifted its head and pricked up its ears at its name. Then, seeing it wasn't needed, it bent down again to the hay.

'I don't think so,' said Koenig.

The fire was warm. Katta could feel the heat of it on her face. Her skirt was still soaked from the river.

It began to steam as it dried. She realized how cold and hungry she was.

'What do you want?' she said.

'I want you to tell me what it's all about,' he answered.

He said it as a simple statement of fact and that annoyed her.

'Don't have to tell you a thing,' she said.

She had meant to sound defiant, but even to her own ears the words had only sounded petulant.

'If you tell me,' said Koenig, 'then these people can look after you both until the boy's better – believe me, they're very good at it. If you don't' – he shrugged – 'I just take you back where I found you.'

She saw straight away that she didn't really have any choice. Even if she lied, what would she say? There wasn't that much she could tell him anyway. But it was still something he wanted and that had to be worth keeping.

'How do I know you won't take us back anyway?' she said.

'You don't. But you were right in the wood. He might be worth something. How much all depends on what you tell me, and what I find out. But if you don't tell me anything, then he's worth nothing at all. Just the ride back to where I found you both. And I'm not sure that you really want that.'

Katta looked at the fire, and at the steam rising from the front of her skirt, but she wasn't seeing it. In her mind's eye she could still see the dwarf sitting on Mathias, pressing his thumbs into the boy's eyes; see the moon-faced man with the silver-topped cane. No. She didn't want to go back.

'There's not much to tell,' she said.

'Then there's no point in not telling it,' said Koenig.

10
The Piece of Paper

It was hard to say what dark dreams were tumbling through Mathias's head while he slept, but there were many of them. Sometimes he would call out, but Katta, who stood and watched him, couldn't make sense of anything he said. He had grown hot and feverish and his words were confused. The Burner woman sat beside him, wiping his head with a cloth. She poured something onto it first, held it to his face and made him breathe it in. It smelled bitter as wormwood, and was as black as nightshade. Katta didn't know whether he was being healed or poisoned, but there was little she could do anyway. She stood inside the door and watched. Once or twice, Burner children looked in to see the boy who had been knifed, but Katta stared at them with such hard, implacable hatred that they backed away and didn't come again.

She had told Koenig all that she had seen and done. He had listened to her without saying a word and she was not sure whether he believed her or not, but she didn't care. Then he had got onto the big horse. He had spoken a few words in Burner to the woman before he left, and she had nodded. What he'd said Katta didn't know, but she could guess. When she tried to stand outside the door of the hut, the Burner woman had called her back in. Hearing their voices, one of the men in the clearing had looked up from his work and stood watching until Katta had done what she was told. If she had had any thought of slipping away into the wood, that had been enough to show her that they wouldn't let her.

Besides, there was the boy.

She had nothing to do but wait either for Koenig to come back or for Mathias to wake up. Waiting wasn't something that she was very good at doing. At the inn she'd had to work all day; every single minute was filled. Now she had nothing to do but stand by the door and wonder what this was all about, and she would have to wait if she was going to find out.

As the day wore on, the sky slowly went the colour

of dull lead. Then it began to snow. Large, lazy flakes that feathered through the high branches of the trees and began to settle on the ground beneath. Thinly at first, but steadily more and more until the stacks of chopped wood grew fat with snow. Katta breathed in the air, it felt wet-cold and clean. Only the earthed mounds, hot on the inside, were not white – the flakes of snow vanished the very instant that they touched, as though they were sharp and had sliced straight through.

And Katta had nothing to do but stand, and watch, and wait.

The afternoon was just growing dark when suddenly Mathias sat up. The lamp had been lit in the hut. He stared with wide unseeing eyes into the shadows of the bracken roof above him. Katta hadn't seen him stirring. For a while he watched her as she stood, arms folded, looking out of the door at the falling snow. He didn't know who she was. Then she turned and saw him.

'Am I dead?' he asked in a whisper.

'Not yet,' she said.

The Burner woman heard the sound of their voices. She stopped what she was doing and, going to the bed, gently laid Mathias down again

unprotesting. He was asleep at once.

It was not until the middle of the next morning that he woke again, but this time the fever had broken. His eyes, though sunken, were bright and clear. The Burner woman had made some broth. Katta had eaten hers before Mathias woke. Now she sat beside him while he ate his and told him what had happened in the tunnel, about Koenig and how they had come to be where they were. He listened intently. She watched his grey face as she spoke, desperate to ask him the two questions she most wanted the answer to, but not sure how to choose

124

the moment. In the end the words just slipped out.

'Why did they try to kill you? What were they looking for?'

Mathias glanced quickly at the Burner woman and back at Katta.

'Don't mind her,' said Katta. 'She only speaks in Burner.'

For a moment he didn't say anything. He hadn't yet decided whether to trust her. Then he remembered the dwarf and the tunnel and what she had already done.

'I think they want a bit of paper,' he said. 'I don't know what it's about.'

He told her what he did know – how Gustav had had a secret. How he had found the paper sewn into the old man's coat. How the man with the silver-topped cane had tried to find it. He looked at the Burner woman again, but she hadn't looked up. She was busy in the corner of the hut.

'It's in my coat pocket,' he said. 'Or it was.'

Katta had used the coat as a blanket in the night. Now she picked it up from the floor where she'd slept and made a fuss of spreading it on the bed, tucking it in around Mathias, but as she did so, she put her hand deep down into one pocket and then the other. She sat back down on the edge of the bed and carefully, so that the Burner woman couldn't see, pressed something small and hard into Mathias's hand.

'This?' she said.

He looked at it and nodded. 'I wish I'd never found it,' he said.

She took it from him and slipped it safely into her apron pocket with the stone. They might need that as well before long.

It snowed through the night, but it had stopped before Koenig returned the next morning. Katta watched him arrive. The big horse was steaming as though it had been ridden hard. There was snow on the shoulders of Koenig's coat. He beat it off with his hat as he got down from the saddle. The Burner men were already working, but he didn't stop to talk to them. He walked straight across the clearing towards the hut. When he came in, he saw that Mathias was awake.

Koenig looked cold and hungry. The Burner woman filled a bowl with hot broth and set it at the small table. She tore a loaf of bread in half and gave that to him as well. It wasn't until the very last scrapings were gone that he pushed the bowl away and spoke.

'Who is Doctor Leiter?' he said.

Mathias looked at Katta. She gave the smallest shake of her head.

'I don't know,' he said.

'He seems to know you,' said Koenig. 'He's left money at the inn for anyone who finds you. Quite a lot of money, actually.'

'So you're going to take him back,' said Katta. Her voice was full of contempt.

Koenig smiled. 'No,' he said. 'He hasn't left nearly enough for that. Your tunnel came down on all my things – I've been back to see it. There's no digging them out. Even if there were, they are no good to me now. I can't sell spoiled goods at a profit.' He shook his head. 'No. It would have to be a great deal more than that.'

'How much more?' said Katta.

She could see where Koenig was leading. He would beat Leiter's price up as high as he could, then sell Mathias for that.

But he shook his head and looked at her with bright, intelligent eyes. 'That's the wrong question,' he said. 'The question should be, "Why does he want our young friend back at all?" The story in the stables is that he stole something from this man and you ran away together. So what did he steal that could possibly be worth so much trouble?'

'I didn't steal anything,' said Mathias.

'It's a piece of paper,' said the Burner woman quietly. 'The girl has it in the pocket of her apron.'

Only then, too late, did Katta realize that the woman had understood every word they had said – understood every word, all the time. She had been tricked by a stinking, filthy Burner. She didn't think. She leaped at the woman's face with her fingers crooked but Koenig caught her – which was fortunate because, quick as a snake, the woman had the small sharp knife in her hand. Koenig pushed Katta away roughly.

'Tashka did no more than I asked her to,' he said. 'And she's fed you and seen to your friend. He'd be dead without her. So you stay there and shut up!'

She knew he was right, but she wasn't going to let him see that, thief that he was, setting this woman to spy on her, so she stared right back at him and spat at the woman. It was a mistake. With fierce coal-black eyes the woman stepped towards her, the blade of the knife held flat between her thumb and finger. Koenig put his hand out and touched the woman's arm. She stopped at once. Still holding onto her, he lifted his other hand to Katta and slowly, so there could be no misunderstanding what he meant, he said, 'Don't ever do that to her again, or she will kill you and there will be nothing I can do to stop her. She will wait until I am gone and then, if you are still here, she will kill you. Do you understand?'

'Give it to him,' said Mathias quietly. 'It's more trouble than it's worth.'

Katta looked at Mathias, then at the hard-faced woman, and her mouth was suddenly dry as ash.

'Please,' said Mathias.

Slowly Katta put her hand into the pocket of her apron. She could feel the sharp edge of the stone, hard and heavy. She looked at Koenig, then at the woman again. But there was nothing she could do. She let the stone drop through her fingers and, drawing the folded paper out, gave it to Koenig. He took it from her, and the woman stepped back and put the knife away.

Carefully Koenig teased one end of the paper open, then, where the shaft of light fell through the door onto the tabletop, he unrolled it and flattened it out between his hands. For a while he said nothing. Then he looked up at Mathias.

'Tell me about this piece of paper,' he said.

'Whose is it?'

'It was my grandfather's,' said Mathias.

'Was?'

'He is dead.'

'Do you know what is written on it?'

Mathias shook his head.

'Then come and see,' said Koenig. 'This is what you nearly died for. It must be worth seeing for that alone.'

Mathias didn't move. Koenig held his hand out to him.

'Come on,' he said. 'Come and see.'

'He can't stand,' said Katta.

'He can stand,' said Koenig.

Mathias put his feet on the ground and stood up. He felt so giddy. There was a buzzing in his ears. He shook his head to clear it. Koenig held out his hand and steadied him.

The piece of paper on the table was no wider than a small letter might be, and not as long. It had been torn off halfway, so that the bottom edge was deeply ragged and uneven. It still had the crease marks from where it had been folded tight and sewn into Gustav's coat. There were other marks too that Mathias knew were from when Gustav had put it in his mouth. For a moment he was in the dark stable again beside the dying man, with the dirty straw on the ground and the bowl of milky white water. It was the same piece of paper, he had no doubt about it, but there was something that made no sense, made no sense at all. He picked it up and turned it over, but it was the same.

On both sides, the piece of paper was completely blank.

11
The Torn Edge

'I don't understand,' said Mathias.

He thought that he was missing something obvious and looked at Koenig, expecting to see the answer, but Koenig didn't understand either. He was holding the paper, a puzzled look on his face.

Katta came and stood by the table. 'All the writing's come off,' she said.

Koenig lifted the paper up to the daylight. Each different town made and marked its own paper. Where the light showed through, he could see the watermark of the Guild of Paper Makers for the town in which it had been made, but there wasn't even so much as the ghost of any writing to show that there had ever been anything written on it at all.

'It can't be this that they want,' said Katta. 'It must be something else.'

In that moment it crossed her mind that Mathias had taken something else, something that he hadn't told her about. She looked at him distrustfully, but he shook his head. He knew that whatever this paper was, it was what Gustav hadn't wanted anyone else to find.

'It must have some trick,' he said.

Koenig looked up at him. 'What do you mean?' he said.

Mathias faltered under the scrutiny of those hard grey eyes. 'It's a conjuror's piece of paper,' he said.

He looked at Katta as though she might be able to explain it better, but she didn't know what he meant either.

'He was a conjuror,' he said. 'There must be some trick to it. Maybe you have to hold it in a special way before you can see the writing.'

'How?' said Koenig, tilting the paper so that the light fell onto it at different angles. 'What sort of thing might he have done?'

Mathias frowned. He tried hard to think but nothing would come. He shook his head. 'I don't know. Maybe you have to hold it over a flame.'

It was possible.

Koenig lit the stub of a candle and they watched

as he carefully passed the paper to and fro above the flame. Katta stood waiting for words to appear but nothing happened.

'It's just a bit of paper,' she said contemptuously. 'You want it to be something else, but that's all it is.'

Koenig didn't look up. 'Things aren't always what they seem,' he said. 'You should have learned that lesson by now.'

He turned and spoke in Burner to the woman. Then he listened to her long answer. Katta guessed that he'd asked the woman to tell him what she'd heard Mathias saying and tried to follow it, but the words were just sounds to her. Sometimes Koenig would interrupt with a question, and then the woman would think about it before saying some more. Finally, when she was done, Koenig picked up the piece of paper again and looked at it carefully.

'Maybe it is, maybe it isn't,' he said.

Then Katta had an idea. It came to her so suddenly that it slipped out before she could stop it. 'Maybe it never had writing on it at all,' she said. 'Maybe it's only half—' She shut her mouth tight. But she'd already said enough for Koenig.

'Half,' he said, turning the new idea around in his head.

He put the paper back down on the table so that
the torn, jagged edge that had been at the bottom
was now at the top.

'What if there is another piece,' he said, 'that
matches this tear.' He drew his fingernail along the
odd, ragged line. 'Matches it exactly.'

Katta looked down at the paper. Turned like this,
it did look like the bottom part of something, not
the top part of it at all. Her idea had been that

135

maybe the writing was on the other part, but then why keep the wrong bit, the bit that was blank?

Now, turned the other way, the tear had a meaning. Even if you were in a hurry, you could tear paper much neater than that if you wanted to. This tear was quite deliberately done. Koenig was right. It wasn't just a tear at all. It was meant to match another piece.

'What if it never had writing on it at all,' he said quietly, weighing that thought. 'What if all it was meant to do was fit?'

Mathias had stopped thinking. His shoulder throbbed and his chest ached. All he wanted to do was lie down. 'What good would that be?' he said, and sat on the bed.

Koenig glanced up at Katta. She'd already worked out the answer to that, but she wasn't going to say.

He took a flat leather wallet from inside his riding coat – Katta caught the flash of a fine silk waistcoat beneath. Carefully folding the paper so that the edge was safe, Koenig put it into the wallet.

'That's his,' said Katta fiercely. 'It's not yours to keep.'

'No,' said Koenig, putting the wallet back inside his coat. 'But if his friends come by, they will have a little more trouble taking it from me than they would from him.'

Katta looked at Koenig – at his slate-grey eyes and hard-edged face – and knew that he was more than probably right.

He stood up, put his hat on and buttoned his coat.

'What will you do to us now?' said Mathias.

His head had drooped and he was staring at the floor. Katta put her hand into her apron pocket and gripped the stone.

'Nothing,' said Koenig. He patted the front of his coat where the wallet lay. 'This little riddle needs solving. You have been the cause of more trouble for me than you know. Let's hope this piece of paper turns out to be worth enough to put it all to rights. Then we shall see.'

He went through the door and whistled for the big bay horse to come to him. It trotted out from the shelter of the trees on the other side of the clearing, shaking its head and mane. Mathias felt so very tired. Tashka must have seen. She came across and, laying him down, covered him over with his coat, but as she did so, she didn't take her eyes off Katta, and Katta found herself wishing very much that Koenig had not gone quite yet, and that he had not left her alone with this Burner woman and her sharp knife.

It was very dark and cold. Mathias lay asleep on the small bed, his coat pulled across him. Katta lay on the floor, but it was so cold. In the end she had climbed up onto the bed and, tucking her knees behind Mathias's for warmth, pressed herself as close to him as she could without waking him. But it was a long, miserable night. At some point a Burner man came into the hut and spoke to the woman, but he didn't stay. In the dark, Katta thought she recognized his voice as that of the man who had carried Mathias in. She wondered whether this was his bed and the woman was his wife. After he had gone, the woman had wrapped herself in a thick shawl and fallen asleep in a chair next to the embers of the fire. Katta watched her, not sure whether it was safe to fall asleep, so she stared up into the shadow shapes that flickered against the bracken roof, pinching herself awake when she felt her eyes closing.

'What does it mean?' whispered Mathias.

Katta hadn't realized that he had woken. 'Go to sleep,' she said.

'Do you know?'

'Maybe.'

She was wiser now. She wasn't going to risk the woman hearing. Slowly she lifted her head, but the woman didn't move. She put her lips close to Mathias's ear and spoke in whispers that only he could hear.

'Someone once left something with Tahlmann – he kept the inn: he had to keep it safe and then give it to someone else, but he didn't know who that would be. So that's what they did. They tore a piece of paper in two – Tahlmann kept one half and the man took the other. I was sweeping up. They didn't mind me and I heard it all. Then, weeks later – weeks and weeks – a stranger came and asked for the package. He had the other piece of paper, and Tahlmann put the two together on the table and they fitted just so. So he gave the package to him, and the stranger went away. What if it's like that?'

'But the other piece could be anywhere,' said Mathias. 'I don't know where it is.'

'Maybe that's why they want it,' whispered Katta. 'Maybe they already know where the other piece is.'

'Then why don't they just take whatever it is?'

Katta wasn't sure what the answer to that was, so she said, 'Maybe they can't.'

Mathias didn't say anything for a moment. It made no sense to him. None of it made any sense. Then he turned his head so that he could see the outline of Katta's face in the dark.

'You won't leave me, will you?' he said quietly.

It hadn't occurred to her until then that he was frightened that she might.

In answer, she pulled the coat up so that it was warm around him. 'You can't even stand up,' she said. 'Anyway, I ain't got no choice, have I?'

'But you don't know anything,' he said.

'Know about the piece of paper, don't I? Tahlmann would sell me as quick as quick if he knew that. And this one' – she meant Koenig – 'he ain't goin' to want anyone else to know about it, is he? So he ain't goin' to let me go.'

There was a long silence.

'Do you think he'll hurt us?' said Mathias.

But she already knew the answer to that. 'He'd have done that already if he was going to,' she said. 'He wants to find out what it's all about, doesn't he? I reckon we're safe till he does.'

'Then what?' said Mathias.

'Then we'll find out,' she said.

'Stop whispering and sleep,' said the woman

suddenly.

Katta froze, but she knew that the woman couldn't have heard much, or she'd have let them carry on whispering and said nothing. She didn't want to risk saying anything else though, so she pulled the coat so that it covered her as well and put her head down on the bed.

As she did so, a new thought began quietly talking in her head. What if it – whatever it was – could make a person rich? What if she found it? There had to be doctors, clever men, who could make her well. Even if they cost a lot of money, if she were rich, she could pay them, and they could make her well.

She lay in the dark and listened, and wondered what it would mean to be rich and never to have to wear a padded cap again.

Koenig was gone all the next day. The Burner woman changed the dressing she had put on Mathias's shoulder. He said it felt better, but it was stiff and he didn't try to move it. What seemed to hurt him more were his ribs. When he got out of the bed, he had to walk slowly and carefully like an old man, stopping and resting, taking small, shallow breaths.

Some of the Burner children were playing in the snow, scooping great handfuls of it up, but Katta stayed where she was and spoke to no one. She was trying to decide what to do.

Then Koenig came back.

Whatever other business he had been about, he had found out two things – the name of the town where the paper had come from – the watermark had given him that. He had only had to find someone who knew about things like that. The other was as simple. He had found out where Dr Leiter wanted word to be sent if Mathias was found.

The moment Koenig had found out the one, he knew he could already guess the other. And he was right, because they were one and the same – Felissehaven.

'It is a merchant city,' he said. 'And a port. All fine colleges and buildings. But then, you'll see it.'

They looked at him, not sure what he meant. Katta was the first to understand.

'He can't travel,' she said.

Koenig glanced at the woman, and she gave the smallest nod of her head. 'He can travel,' he said. 'Tashka will see to him.' Then, looking straight at Katta, he added, 'And if you stay here much longer, she will probably see to you as well.'

It might have been a joke, but when Katta glanced quickly at the Burner woman, she saw those cold, dark, vengeful eyes, and wasn't so sure that it was. Besides, she had made up her mind – she wanted to be rich, and if that meant going with Koenig, then that is what she would do. At least until they had found out what the paper meant, and then they'd just have to take their chance.

The following day he gave them thick Burner coats and leather boots. Katta didn't understand what hold he had over the Burners, but they did what he asked willingly and without question.

They were almost ready to leave when it happened.

Koenig was on the big horse saying his farewells. Mathias sat in the saddle in front of him. Katta was going to have to walk. Just as they were turning to leave, a Burner boy joined them. He was taller than she was, but not much older. He already wore a pack of his own. It seemed that he was coming too, though Koenig hadn't said anything about it. Katta watched him sling the saddlebags he carried over the back of the horse, and an empty feeling began to crawl slowly into her stomach. She couldn't take her

143

eyes off him. That face was fixed in her memory as clearly as if it had been scratched into steel. He was older, it was true, but there was no mistaking it.

It was the boy who had thrown the stone.

12
The Tracks in the Snow

Katta felt weak. It was as though, without her knowing it, someone had stepped inside her and drained out every spark of life. She stood numbly, staring at the boy. He was adjusting the straps on his pack. When he turned round, he looked straight through her. There was not the faintest sign that he knew who she was, but she knew him. How could she ever forget?

Hatred of this boy had filled her life. She had never been able to let go of it. Each time she woke, soiled and filthy, on the floor, or took off the cap to wash her long, beautiful hair – being careful of the place where the stone had hit her, leaving the bone broken and eggshell-thin – she thought of him. Thought, over and over again, of what she would do to him if she ever found him. Heaven help him if she did. She wouldn't kill him – that would be too easy for him. She would do something that he would have to live with, just like she did. It would have to be something that would ruin his life as he had ruined hers, and he wouldn't ever know why it had been done to him. She wouldn't tell him. He would have to live with the awful unfairness of it, just as she did.

That hatred went round and round in her head, buzzing like a malignant bee, until finally she'd decided what she would do if she ever found him – she'd blind him.

He would have to live with his darkness, just like she did with hers. It wouldn't be hard to do. She had done the thing in her head, imagined it so many times that it was easy. He would be asleep, and she would creep up quietly without waking him and slit a knife across both his eyes before he could even twitch. It would be as simple as that.

That is what she would do.

And now, here he was.

But she didn't feel like she imagined she would, seeing him delivered into her hands. The reality of it was all too enormous to understand. So she just stared numbly at the boy and at the thick snow and

146

the white trees beyond. Then Koenig was walking his horse out of the clearing, calling to them to follow, and she had to go.

Beneath the cover of the trees the snow lay banked in drifts. There was no path to follow; they had to make their own. Even walking in the steps of the big horse it was hard work. The coat Katta had been given by the Burners was thick and warm, and soon she was hot and cross and tired, but for all her complaining they didn't stop. Koenig walked the horse on and she and the boy followed as best they could. The boy didn't seem to mind. He walked steadily through the snow. Once or twice Katta lost her balance and fell, but she wouldn't have him touch her. He stood with his hand out to help, but she wouldn't take it and he'd shrugged, but still waited until she had got herself to her feet before he went on. Then she had walked behind him, staring at his back and hating him. Not sure whether she hated him more for what he had done to her, or for being oblivious to the fact that he had even done it.

Mathias sat in front of Koenig, the movement of the horse rocking him to sleep. Tashka had given him something to drink before they left. It had made him feel warm and deadened the pain. He

watched the quiet, white woods pass by as though he were being drawn slowly through them on a ribbon of thick velvet.

Koenig hardly spoke at all. Sometimes he asked Mathias a question to do with Gustav or Leiter or the circus, and then he was quiet again. It was as though he were turning the answers over in his head, slowly making sense of it all.

They stopped to rest. Koenig had food, which he shared out between them.

'Who's he?' said Katta. The boy was sitting with Mathias. 'He to spy on us, like the other one?'

'Do you want any food?' said Koenig. He held onto the bread he had been going to give her. 'Because if you do, you need to have better manners than that.'

'Then I don't think I want any,' she said.

She had walked all morning and was as hungry as could be, but she wasn't going to say. She watched as Koenig put the bread back into his bag.

'His name is Stefan,' he said.

'Why's he here?'

Koenig turned away without bothering to answer her and walked over to where the two boys sat. With his knife, Stefan was cutting a piece of cold meat for Mathias.

'How is arm?' Stefan said.

He spoke the words with so thick an accent that Mathias was not sure what he had said, and Stefan frowned as though he wasn't certain that he had said the right words anyway, so he touched his own shoulder and then Mathias knew what he had meant.

He nodded. 'It's all right,' he said.

'*Gut*,' said Stefan, smiled and gave Mathias the meat.

He folded his knife shut and put it back into his

pack. Katta watched him do it. She was angry with Mathias in a way that she couldn't have described, because he was speaking to the boy. Angry with herself because she was hungry and could have had food. Frightened about what she was going to do next.

They did not rest for long. Koenig put Mathias back into the saddle, then climbed up. Stefan smiled at Katta, but she walked past him.

They had gone on for an hour or so when the horse suddenly stopped, its ears pricked. It turned its head and looked back over its shoulder, the way they had come. It snorted and walked on, but then stopped again.

'Steady, Razor,' said Koenig, and the horse tossed its head.

They walked on once more, but a change had come over Koenig and the horse – Mathias could feel it. They were taut and alert. Koenig had let Stefan and Katta trail behind, but now he slowed so that they could catch up.

'What is it?' said Mathias.

'Nothing to be bothered about,' said Koenig. 'Probably just wolves.'

'Wolves!'

Koenig grinned at him. 'Let's see how many there are before we get worried.'

There were still a couple of hours of daylight left. They rode on for what seemed quite a while. Then Koenig stopped again. He looped the reins over the horse's neck and climbed down.

There were tracks in the snow. Mathias looked down at them, and suddenly they made sense.

'They're our tracks,' he said. 'We've gone round in a circle.'

Koenig was casting about, looking carefully at the ground. Stefan took off his pack, dropped it in the snow, and came and stood by him.

'*Wolfen?*' Stefan said.

Koenig shook his head. '*Ney*,' he said, but he sounded puzzled. '*Voye.*' He pointed to the ground in one place, and then again in another, showing Stefan what he had seen in the snow.

'What is it?' said Mathias.

Koenig straightened up and looked along the line of their old tracks that led away into the wood. 'We're being followed,' he said.

Then Mathias understood what Koenig had done. He had taken them round in a great circle, to cross their own tracks and the tracks of whatever was

151

behind them. But it wasn't wolves, and he suddenly realized that Koenig must have known that all along.

Koenig stood in the snow beside the big horse. He put his boot by one of the marks and frowned. It was the print of a boot, too small for a man, too large and deep for a child. It followed the line of their tracks exactly – there was no mistaking that.

He shook his head again. 'Whoever it is, there's only one of them,' he said.

'They might just be following in our tracks because it's easier,' said Mathias. 'Stefan and Katta are.'

'Maybe,' said Koenig, but he didn't sound as though he believed it.

He gathered the reins one handed, and swung himself back up into the saddle. Stefan trod through the snow to where he had dropped his pack and picked it up. Mathias felt suddenly cold inside. He looked at Katta, but she had her back to him and was fastening her coat. There was only one person Mathias had ever met who was smaller than a man but larger than a child. But it couldn't be. He shivered.

It was an uneasy thought and it persisted, growing on Mathias as the light began to fade and the shadows beneath the trees began to darken. They had left the thick wood and come out onto a dirt road. The snow was marked with cart tracks, as though several things had already passed that way, but it was empty now, and it had begun to snow again – small icy spicules that wandered aimlessly in the air.

They were going to find an inn – Koenig had said that, but little else. Only once had he stopped and, standing up in his stirrups, looked back the way they had come, but the track was empty for as far as he could see, and he had ridden on again. Only Mathias kept looking. Finally Koenig said, 'You won't see him, whoever he is.'

'I might.'

'No,' said Koenig. 'Not if he was following us, you won't. His tracks will have crossed ours again, where we stopped. Now he understands that we know he is there. So he has to be careful or he will get a pistol ball through his skull. You won't see him if he is clever, and if he is not clever, he is dead.'

Mathias looked behind again, the feeling of unease becoming the first cold fingers of fear.

Koenig chuckled. 'Don't worry yourself,' he said lightly. 'I said *you* might not see him – but I will.'

If someone else had said that, Mathias would have thought it just an empty brag. But not Koenig. He wondered how many men Koenig had killed. How many had tried to kill him and not lived to see another day.

'Besides,' said Koenig, 'there's the inn.'

In the distance in front of them Mathias could see the pinprick light of a lamp. Behind them the road was empty; small flakes of snow wandered and disappeared into the falling dark. Whoever was following them was out there. Mathias shivered again and pulled up the collar of his coat.

The inn smelled of all the things Katta knew so well, as though they were grimed into her skin: pipe smoke and beer, wood smoke and stale cooking. The smell of travelling men and damp clothes. The big downstairs room was already full. There was a murmur of talk, a fire roaring against one wall. Katta watched the girls carrying laden trays of drink. She might have been looking at herself. People hardly spared them a glance as they came in. Koenig found the innkeeper and paid for a room, then they were taken upstairs. Katta looked at the girl who showed them the way and felt again that same queer sense of watching herself.

'What's it like here?' she said to the girl, but the girl didn't answer.

There was a fire lit in their room and Koenig had food brought up. Stefan couldn't find his knife to cut his meat with – it must have dropped out of his pack in the forest – so Koenig cut it for him and scolded him for losing something he might need. The two of them talked in Burner. Mathias ate his food and then lay down on the big curtained bed. There was only one, but it was large enough for them all if they slept two at each end. His shoulder and ribs ached. Koenig took a small flask from his coat, poured the liquid into its cap and had Mathias drink. It was the same thing that Tashka had given him that morning. It numbed the pain and made him feel warm and drowsy. He put his head onto the dirty pillow and felt sleep begin to creep over him.

Katta sat in the firelight and watched Koenig and Stefan talking.

In the pocket of her apron was Stefan's knife.

13
The Fight at the Inn

No one had seen her take it. It had been easy. They were all looking at the marks in the snow. She slipped her hand into Stefan's pack and put the knife in her own pocket. When she was quite sure they hadn't seen, she undid her coat and quickly dropped the knife into her apron, then fastened her coat again, and that was all Mathias had seen her doing. But now she had the boy, and a knife.

'Are you sulking still?' said Koenig.

Katta looked up. 'I'm not hungry,' she said.

'You must eat, or you won't be able to last tomorrow.'

'Maybe I won't have to.'

There was something in the tone of her voice that could not be missed and Koenig looked at her with those deep-seeing eyes of his. If she was not careful, she thought, he would guess that she had the knife.

'What are we going to do in Felissehaven?' she said quickly.

But he was too sharp for that. She could feel his gaze upon her even though she was looking away, looking at the fire, looking anywhere but at him.

'Let's get there first, shall we?' he said. 'Without too much trouble, that is.'

'Can't wait,' she said.

Koenig had taken off his thick riding coat. Now he might have been a gentleman, with his fine scarf wound around his throat, his silk waistcoat and black stuff jacket. He opened the saddlebags that he had laid across the back of a chair and took from them two pistols. He checked each, and then pushed one down inside his jacket where it could not be seen. 'I'm going to see if our friend has arrived downstairs,' he said.

He tossed the other pistol to Stefan, who caught it awkwardly. It looked large and clumsy in his hands.

'Can't be too careful,' he said. 'Stay here. Don't open the door to anyone but me. Don't go outside. Do you understand?'

'Or he'll shoot us?' said Katta mockingly.

'No,' said Koenig. 'But he will shoot anyone else

who tries to come in.' His voice was deadly serious. 'Now isn't the time to play games, Katta.'

It was the first time he had used her name, and it startled her. He must have heard Mathias say it a dozen times, but he hadn't spoken it until now.

'No games, Katta,' he said.

Then he stepped into the hall and closed the door behind him.

'What did he mean?' said Mathias sleepily from the bed. He'd heard the words but they'd come to him slowly and fuzzily, as though from a long way off.

'Nothing,' she said. 'Get some sleep. I'll stay awake.'

She watched Mathias close his eyes.

Now it was just her and the boy.

Down in the quiet of the stables, the horses shifted their feet uneasily as something disturbed them, a small square shape slipping from shadow to shadow across the yard. The big horse lifted its head, pricked its ears and snorted.

'Why don't you lie down?' said Katta.

Stefan was sitting in a chair by the fire; he had turned it so that it faced the door. He had the pistol on his lap. He looked up at her, a little surprised. It was the first time she'd spoken to him. She put her hands together like a pillow against her cheek.

'Sleep,' she said and pointed to him. 'You sleep now. I'll watch.'

'I watch,' said Stefan.

'Not for much longer, you won't,' said Katta under her breath. 'I'll sleep then,' she said, pointing to her chest. 'Me.'

Stefan nodded, and Katta climbed onto the bed. She closed her eyes, but she wasn't asleep. She lay there with her eyes shut and listened to the buzzing of the bee in her head.

Koenig sat at a table close to the fire. He wasn't alone. He had found a place next to two gentlemen and their lady companions. The ladies had their hair piled up in the fashionable way. They had all travelled together in the same carriage. Koenig listened to their empty chatter, but all the while he watched the room, saw who came in and went out. When one of the girls with her empty tray passed him, he stopped her.

'I was expecting a friend,' he said. 'A short man. He's been walking, no horse to stable. Has he come yet?'

This girl would know. He had chosen one he had seen when they arrived, so he knew she would have noticed anyone who had come after them.

She looked about. 'That him?' she said.

She pointed across the room to a small fat man who was smoking a pipe. He had a small fat wife beside him.

'No,' said Koenig.

'Only one I've seen,' she said.

One of the ladies touched his arm. 'Do you play cards, sir?' she said.

'Never for money,' said Koenig.

She smiled at him. 'Perhaps we could play then?'

She rapped her fan on the table. 'Cards, everyone!' she said. 'Our new companion can deal.'

She laid her hand on his arm again. 'I'm sure I can trust you to play fairly,' she said.

Up in the room Katta was watching Stefan. He had settled in the chair and the warmth of the fire was making him drowsy. It had been a long, cold day and they had walked so far. Sometimes his head would nod, but then he'd lift it again and stretch and blink, trying to keep awake. Then the warmth would work upon him, and after a while his eyes would close.

Katta said nothing. But she watched like a hawk, barely breathing, not making a sound, not moving a muscle. Finally his head drooped and he didn't lift it. For all that he had tried not to, for all that Koenig had left him to watch, Stefan was asleep.

Very slowly, not taking her eyes off him, Katta sat up in the bed. She looked at Mathias. His eyes were shut and he was breathing deeply and evenly. Carefully she put her hand into her apron and took out the knife. It felt hard and heavy. It was folded shut. Just as carefully, she opened it. The blade was sharp; it felt cold against her hand. The light of the flames from the fire danced along it. It was how she had always imagined it – the boy sleeping, not knowing what was about to happen to him, the knife in her hand. But it was not the same at all.

It was real.

All those other, imagined times fell away from her like the paper-thin things they were, and she was left with a real knife and a real boy. How could she do it? It was so wrong. But then, what he had done was wrong too. But he hadn't known he'd done it. But he'd thrown the stone, hadn't he? He must have meant to hurt someone – he'd meant that, and it had been her he'd hurt. That's what he'd done. But maybe he hadn't really meant it at all?

She sat statue-still while the different thoughts raced in her head. But slowly one thought gained the upper hand, pushing all the others aside. She had sworn that she would do this to him if she ever found him. It would be like a broken promise if she didn't. As if she were a coward. It didn't matter that it was wrong. She had sworn that she would do it, so that is what she was going to do.

Quietly she put her feet on the floor and, not making a sound, stood up. Very slowly she began to move towards him. The firelight flickered and her shadow stretched back across the room. She bent down and reached one hand forward to take the pistol from his lap, but his hand was resting on it and she hesitated, drew back and edged around his chair so that she stood behind him. Then she reached her hand over his head and brought the knife down until the blade rested in front of his eyes. She could feel her heart pounding; she was shaking.

'Katta! No!'

Mathias had sat up in bed: he was awake, staring at her with wide eyes. As Stefan jerked his head and opened his eyes, Katta drew the blade across them. But he'd moved enough – the blade sliced across his forehead, deep as the bone, and suddenly there was blood everywhere as he stumbled from the chair.

'Katta!' shouted Mathias.

She stood staring in disbelief at the knife in her hands, and realized what she had done. Stefan had his hands to his face; there was blood coming between his fingers. He couldn't see – he blundered into the table and fell. Mathias was out of the bed in a flash, arm tight across his chest, trying to reach Stefan before Katta did. His face was shocked and white.

'What have you done?'

Stefan was whimpering; he was pressing himself against the bed, trying to get away from Katta, but she didn't move. She dropped the knife. What had she done? All those years of impotent hate burst inside her.

'He did it to me!' she screamed, her eyes full of tears.

Mathias looked blankly up at her.

'This!' she shouted and, grabbing her cap, pulled it off her head and threw it at him as hard as she could. Her hair was red in the firelight.

'He did it to me!' she shouted. 'It was him!'

She stabbed her fingers to the place in her head. Parted the hair so that he could see the bone.

'This! He did it to me.'

Mathias didn't understand. She had never told him. He stared uncomprehendingly from her to the boy. There was blood everywhere.

Katta put her hands to her head and ran. The door to the room was shut and bolted; she drew the bolt and flung it open. She didn't know where she was going – she ran blindly down the narrow passages and turns, not seeing, not stopping until, coming round a corner, she looked down into the half-light and froze.

Climbing in through a window at the end of the passageway in front of her was Valter.

She let out a scream, stifling it at once. But it was too late – that was enough. He hadn't seen her until then. He was already halfway through the window; he turned his head and looked right at her.

She didn't wait. She turned and fled back the way she had come, but she wasn't sure which way it was. There was a small flight of steps – had she come down it? She couldn't remember. She took them two at a time and ran along the passage, shouting at the top of her voice.

'Mathias! Mathias!'

The door to the room was still open; she came through it at a run and slammed it, bolting it behind her. Stefan now had a sheet to his head: Mathias was holding it, trying to staunch the blood. When they saw her, they both flinched; Stefan backed away. She slid the bolt home in the door.

'Get the pistol!' she shouted.

Neither Mathias nor Stefan moved.

'It's him!'

Desperately she began looking for where the pistol had fallen from Stefan's lap. She saw it under the table, got down on her hands and knees and was scrabbling for it as the door bent inwards and the frame cracked. She stared, horrified; outside Valter put his shoulder to the door again. It bent further and this time, in a splintering of wood, the bolt gave way.

He was a terrible sight. He had been burned and buried. He stood with his arms wide, ready to catch them if they ran.

'Where is it?' he hissed.

Katta had the pistol in her hands. She had never used one before, not even held one. It was so heavy. She didn't know what to do. She pulled the hammer back with her hand like she'd seen people do; it was hard, but it locked with a click. Still crouching, she raised the pistol at Valter and pulled the trigger. There was a flash and it fired. The sound was deafening in the small space – plaster showered from the ceiling behind Valter where the ball struck – but it had missed him completely. With a yell, he leaped at Mathias, who jumped up onto the bed one side and down the other.

Stefan was in the way; he didn't seem to understand what was happening. Valter caught hold of him and, with the back of his hand, gave him one enormous blow across his face. It sent Stefan crashing into the wall; he slid down it to the floor, then didn't move. Valter fixed his eyes on Mathias, who stood with the bed between them.

'Where is it, little boy?' he said.

'He can't catch us both,' said Katta. 'He can only get one.'

An iron poker was leaning against the fireplace – it wasn't much, but it was something. Dropping the pistol, she grabbed at the poker and held it unsteadily in both hands. Valter smiled. This was going to be a good game. He drew his long knife from his coat and moved slowly towards her; she circled round the table, keeping it between them. It was now or not at all.

'Run!' she shouted, and swung at Valter's head with the poker. She missed; he caught the end of it one-handed and jerked it away from her. But Mathias had already leaped onto the bed and down the other side. The dwarf leaped after him, slashing at him with his knife, but he only caught the curtains that hung around the bed. They ripped and fell, and in that moment's confusion, as Valter wrestled himself free of the heavy folds of cloth, Katta and Mathias were through the door and down the passage. But they had only a moment's start before the dwarf was after them. They could hear him coming. They ran, but he was too quick for them. He caught hold of Mathias by the back of his neck and slammed his head into the wall. Mathias dropped like a sack. Katta turned round to face him.

Valter was standing over Mathias with his knife drawn – when Koenig shot him.

14
What Katta Had to Do

Koenig had heard the crack of Katta's pistol shot. Everybody had. But only he had known what it meant. He was out of his chair and, not caring who got in his way, across the crowded room before anyone else had moved. He took the stairs at a run, the cocked pistol already in his hand.

The door of the room had been broken in. Stefan was lying in a heap against one wall. Koenig knelt and turned him over. The boy was unconscious. He had a deep wound across his forehead and his face was a mask of blood. Koenig took in the disorder – the table overturned, the bed hangings pulled down – but of Mathias and Katta there was no sign.

He swore.

They hadn't passed him, so he knew they must have gone the other way. He ran back through the door and down the empty passage. Even as he did so, he heard the thump of Mathias's head against the wall and Katta's gasp of breath.

Then he turned the corner.

As Valter heard the sound of Koenig behind him, he let go of Mathias's hair and, twisting round in one liquid movement, stood grinning, knife ready in his hand—

And Koenig shot him.

The pistol ball caught the dwarf in the middle of his chest. It lifted him clean off his feet and smashed him into the window behind. In a shower of breaking glass the frame gave way and Valter went backwards into the dark, snow-filled courtyard below.

For an instant none of them moved. Koenig stood with the smoking pistol levelled at the place where Valter had been, then slowly he let his arm drop. Katta closed her eyes, her heart hammering in her chest. Mathias lay staring at the ceiling, breathing in snatched gasps. Koenig stepped over him and, leaning out of the broken window, looked down into the courtyard.

But there was no one there.

He craned his head out, looking both ways along

the length of the wall, trying to see where the dwarf had crawled to before he'd died. But there was no sign of him at all. Just a line of freshly made tracks disappearing into the darkness.

Other people were arriving now, crowding into the passage behind Koenig, wanting to know what had happened. He turned and pushed his way through them, ignoring all their questions. The boy and the girl were safe enough for the moment. He had to see to Stefan.

Katta stood there, dazed, the deafening sound of the pistol shot ringing in her head. Everything had happened so quickly.

A wind was blowing through the broken window. It was wet with snow. A man in a blue coat was asking her if she was hurt, but she barely heard him.

She was shaking.

She knelt down beside Mathias and put her hand against his face. His eyes were wide with terror.

'It's all right,' she said. 'He's gone.'

He looked up at her, but he didn't really see her. He could still see the face of the dwarf and the long silver knife.

'It's all right,' she said.

She put her arms around him and held him while

171

the people crowded about them and stared.

Someone lifted her up. They set her on her feet. It was the man in the blue coat. He bent down and picked up Mathias in his arms, then carried him back along the passage, up the small flight of steps to the room with the broken-in door.

Dumbly Katta followed him.

Koenig had already lifted Stefan onto the bed. He'd torn a sheet into lengths and was trying to stop the blood. Stefan was lolling like a rag doll. Katta had never needed to think about what she'd do after she'd blinded the boy. There had only ever been the blinding, and nothing else. But this was real and there was so much blood.

She felt sick.

Koenig turned and saw the man carrying Mathias. 'Is he hurt?' he said.

Katta couldn't say anything. She was still staring at Stefan.

'Is he hurt?' asked Koenig again.

The words shook her awake. 'Yes,' she said.

Koenig took her hand, stuffed the wad of torn sheet into it and pressed it against Stefan's head. 'Press it hard,' he said.

Then, taking Mathias from the man, he set him

down on the edge of the bed. Mathias moaned.

Stefan was completely senseless. She had to hold him upright. But she could see what she'd done to him now. Right across his forehead was a cut down to the bone – she could see the white of it. If Mathias hadn't woken him when he did, the blade would have gone through both his eyes like a razor.

The thought of what that would have done stuffed the breath up inside her. How could she have thought she could do that?

She pressed the torn wad of sheet to Stefan's head, but the blood just kept coming. She looked up, imploring someone to help.

The man in the blue coat reached down and took the sodden cloth from her hand. There was a water jug beside the bed. He flicked his head towards it. 'Get some more,' he said. 'Go on.'

Still shaking, she picked up the jug and, pushing her way through the crowd of people that were gawping at the doorway, stepped out into the passage and took a deep gulp of breath and then another.

Downstairs the inn was astir. Some men had taken lanterns and gone looking outside, but the tracks they found in the snow led straight into the dark forest. No one was going to follow them in there. There was little more that could be done. Snow was falling. By daylight the tracks would be covered over and that had to be an end of it.

Katta made her way down the stairs. The air was thick with pipe smoke and the smell of people. One of the girls showed her to the water pump in a dark stone room at the back of the inn.

At the top of the steps that led down to it, Katta stopped. On the far side of the little room, a door led to the outside world. It was bolted fast, but it buffeted on its hinges as the wind blew and she could see that it wasn't locked.

If she filled the jug and went back upstairs, Stefan would tell Koenig what she'd done. And then what?

Or she could steal a coat and slip away through that door. No one was watching. They wouldn't even know she'd gone. They'd never find her. There had to be a hundred places she could hide.

She put the jug down on the floor and looked back over her shoulder to where the coats were hung to dry. It would be so easy to take one. But if she did, she'd be leaving Mathias behind and suddenly, in ways that she couldn't even begin to explain, that seemed a much worse thing to do.

She stood with her back against the wall, looking at the door and at the coats, but she just couldn't do it. It was always that same thought that stopped her.

Mathias.

Taking a deep breath, she picked up the jug again and filled it.

When she got back to the upstairs room, several things had changed. The man in the blue coat had gone and there were no people in the doorway and that wasn't good. She'd counted on there being other people there. Stefan had been laid down on the bed and for one wild moment, not of guilt but relief, she thought that he was dead and that she was safe. But then she realized that, like Tashka had done to Mathias, Koenig must have given Stefan some drug to make him sleep. He'd smeared the cut with that same thick black paste, and it had stopped bleeding.

She put the jug of water down beside the bed. She could feel Mathias watching her, but she couldn't look at him. A confusion of thoughts was rushing through her head. If she could find the knife, she could throw it away – maybe drop it out of the window into the snow – and then Koenig would never know. But that was no good, because Stefan would still tell as soon as he woke up. She cast her eyes about the floor for the knife, but she couldn't see it anywhere. It must have been kicked beneath the bed or under the large wooden chest that stood against the wall. Her cap lay where she'd thrown it. She picked it up.

Koenig had wiped his hands clean on a piece of torn sheet and was setting the upturned table back on its legs. He put the chair next to it. As he did so, something caught his eye. Katta saw it too.

On the floor where the table had lain was Stefan's knife.

Koenig bent down and picked it up. He knew whose knife it was. There was blood on the blade. He turned and looked at Katta. There was no going back now and she knew it.

'I cut him,' she said.

How could she even begin to explain? She was still holding her leather cap. She held it out towards Koenig, but her hand was shaking.

'He's why I wear this,' she said. 'Why I wear it every stinking minute of every stinking day.' Her eyes were filling with angry tears. 'It was him what done it. He threw the stone. I knowed it the minute

I saw him, so I took his knife and I cut him, and you can do what you like, 'cos I don't care.'

She stood there, her face so fierce that Mathias thought she was going to try and fight. He didn't know what he could do if she did. But Koenig didn't move. He didn't take his eyes from her.

'You could have said.'

'Yeah, well, I didn't.'

His eyes never leaving her, he carefully wiped the sharp blade of the knife, then folded it shut with a click. 'Let me give you some advice, girl,' he said slowly in a cold, dangerous whisper. 'Never do anything out of revenge. Once you start, it will never let you go. Believe me, I know.'

He put the knife in his pocket, still looking at her with those hard, slate-grey eyes. 'You've had your blood,' he said. 'Don't even think about taking any more.'

He pushed the hand that held the cap away. 'Put it back on,' he said.

In the night, snow fell. By the morning it had buried the road through the forest in an impassable deep, white drift. There was no leaving the inn now, even had they wanted to. When Stefan woke, Koenig had spoken to him, but what he'd said Katta didn't know and she wasn't going to ask. Stefan watched her darkly as she moved about, and she pretended not to notice him doing it.

She tried to keep her distance from him. She took herself downstairs and stood in the doorway of the small snug room behind the bar, watching the two fine ladies playing cards and backgammon in front of the fire. When they saw her, they gave her little pieces of cut apple to eat, as though she were a pet. She wondered what it must be like to be a lady and dress in silks and satins. When she went back to the room, she tried to walk as she imagined a fine lady might walk, but the serving girls saw her on the stairs and laughed. They knew their own sort when they saw it. Any other time and she'd have slapped their faces for them, but not now. She'd seen enough blood already.

It was another day before they could leave the inn. By then the ladies were leaving as well. They said that Katta, Mathias and Stefan could ride with them for a while in their coach. They weren't going to Felissehaven, but at least part of their journey lay the same way. Katta couldn't believe it. Her face shone with excitement. It was as though she had forgotten everything else. She combed her hair and tidied her clothes. When the time came, she stepped into the small coach and sat like a queen, her hands folded in her lap. Mathias took the place next to her and Stefan pressed himself into the furthest corner, where he sat watching Katta in brooding silence.

Koenig rode behind the coach with the two gentlemen. They had hired horses for themselves at the inn. Koenig's big horse towered over them both. Mathias thought that he looked more like a highwayman now than a gentleman. Perhaps the two men thought so too because they didn't look at all comfortable with the arrangement. Or perhaps that was just because they weren't riding in the coach.

As the coach rolled out into the deep snow, Koenig's big horse suddenly pricked its ears and stopped dead. Koenig patted its huge neck and followed its gaze out into the silent, snow-covered trees, but he could see nothing.

'Steady, Razor,' he said quietly.

The horse shook its mane and reluctantly walked on.

But it had been right.

From the deep cover of the trees, Valter watched them go.

15

The Road to Felissehaven

Anna-Maria sat beside Lutsmann as he drove the
creaking cart along the road that led through the
woods.

It had taken them a whole day to set off after
Leiter. The tavern keeper had laid hold of their
bone-thin horses against the cost of burying Gustav,
and Lutsmann had been given no option but to pay.
Anna-Maria had stood swearing at the man, white
with rage, and the price had gone up with virtually
every word she spat out at him. Had she hit him with
her riding crop, as she almost did, they wouldn't
have got the horses back at all.

By the time they arrived at Katta's inn – the one
Leiter had taken Mathias to – Leiter had gone. But
all was not lost. If it wasn't clear to Lutsmann, it was
clear to Anna-Maria that whatever it was that Leiter

wanted, he hadn't found it, otherwise he wouldn't have left the promise of money – a large amount of money – for whoever found Mathias. And what was it that Mathias was supposed to have stolen?

That was just smoke.

All this was turning over in Anna-Maria's mind as she watched the leather of the reins along the back of the horses. Lutsmann could almost hear her thinking.

'My plum?' he said.

'We should never have sold him.'

Lutsmann knew better than to remind her it had been *her* idea that they should.

'Maybe we could buy him back?' he said.

She looked at him darkly. 'Dolt!'

But then her expression changed. It became cunning. 'Or maybe we could help look for him,' she said. 'Without us Doctor Leiter might be sent any boy. But we know him. Know his little ways.'

'We were especially fond of him, I recall,' said Lutsmann.

'Loved him as though he were our own son,' said Anna-Maria.

'And . . .' Lutsmann paused. 'If we do find him, my dear . . . ?' he said uncertainly.

world, not part of it at all. He couldn't feel the tips of his fingers and his tongue was fat in his mouth. He didn't like it at all, but his chest hurt too much not to drink each capful when Koenig poured it.

In the few days they had walked, Stefan's mood had become even more sullen and black. He didn't always answer Koenig when he spoke to him and he didn't try to talk to Mathias. If Katta caught his eye, he'd stare at her until she turned away. It wasn't so much that she couldn't meet his look – she could outstare a cat – it was the sight of the deep, ugly wound the width of his forehead. It was going to scar him all his life. It was what people would notice about him before anything else; what they'd remember about him afterwards. But she felt no satisfaction. It wasn't how she thought she'd feel. If she felt anything, it was shame, and she couldn't explain why that should be. Not after what he had done to her. But when she thought of what would have happened had Mathias not woken him up when he did, all her breath stopped inside.

But Stefan knew none of that. All he knew was what Koenig had told him, and that didn't mean anything. He couldn't remember her. He didn't care if it had been him that had hurt her. He'd seen the mirror on the wall and what she'd done to his face and that was all that mattered.

Koenig had given him his knife back. Katta wished he hadn't done that. She wondered if she could steal it like she'd done before, but Stefan had made that mistake once and he wasn't going to let it happen again. He kept the knife tucked inside his shirt. But each time he used it, he looked at Katta and turned the blade over in his hands, and she understood what he meant.

It was what Koenig had told her. Revenge follows you.

She didn't think Stefan would try to hurt her while Koenig was there, but she didn't trust him any more than that. Worse, she knew that it was her own fault, but there was no going back now. She would have to take very great care, and the first thing to do, she decided, was to stay as close to Koenig as she could. Besides, she wanted to know what he was going to do next.

But for now she walked beside Mathias, keeping pace with him, letting him lean on her, which made her feel warm in ways that she didn't really under-stand either.

'Did he ever learn you any of it?' she asked him.

185

'Tricks and stuff?'

She meant Gustav. She loved the idea of the magic show. But Mathias shook his head.

'He should have learned it you,' she said. 'Then you could have done it together.'

Koenig had been listening to them talk. He looked down at Katta from the saddle. 'Maybe that's just what he didn't want,' he said. 'Maybe that's all your piece of paper really is. The tricks an old man didn't want anyone else to know.'

Mathias looked up at him. He didn't believe for a moment that Koenig thought that. 'You don't think it is,' he said.

Koenig stood up in his stirrups and looked back along the road. Then he sat down in the saddle again. 'No,' he said. 'People don't die just for that.'

He looked down at Mathias as though he were about to say more, but then the expression on his face changed; it became one of concern. Mathias turned to see what it was that he was looking at. He hadn't noticed that Katta had stopped walking, but she had. She was standing quite still, staring blankly, her face pale.

'Katta?' he said.

But she didn't hear him, because inside her head

the world was breaking into a thousand little pinpricks of light. A thin noise was coming from between her teeth.

Before Mathias could do anything, she pitched forward into the snow, kicking and jerking like some broken puppet. The sudden violence of it sent the big horse dancing sideways across the track. Stefan thought it was a trick. He fumbled with the buttons of his coat, pulling the knife from inside his shirt and shouting at her to get up. But then he saw the red froth around her lips where she'd bitten her tongue, and her eyes wide and staring. Koenig reined in the horse and dropped from the saddle into the snow. He caught hold of Katta's head, cupping it in his hands as she beat it on the ground.

There was nothing Mathias could do but stand and watch.

It seemed to last an age. Koenig held onto her until at last she stopped kicking; then he put his hat in the snow and, brushing the hair from her face, carefully laid her head on it like a pillow. It was several moments before she opened her eyes. When she did, she stared slowly about her, blinking, as though she didn't know where she was or what had happened.

Then, very quietly, she began to cry.

Stefan stood staring down at her. There was blood and spit all over her face. She'd wet herself too. Mathias knelt down in the snow and looked up at Stefan. It was an accusation and Stefan knew it.

'She sick!' he shouted. He held his hair back to show the thick ugly cut. 'She do this!'

Katta slowly looked up at him, her face wet with tears, her eyes barely focusing. But she knew who it was. 'I hate you,' she said.

He swore at her in Burner, but Koenig put out his hand and pushed him away. Stefan spat angrily in the snow and, kicking at it, walked off towards where the horse stood with its reins loose about its neck.

Koenig knelt down beside her. 'Can you sit on a horse?' he said quietly.

She nodded her head almost imperceptibly, but even that hurt.

He helped her to stand up, then put his arm around her and lifted her into the saddle. With Mathias beside him, he made the horse walk on, holding onto her stirrup so that she wouldn't fall. Stefan stood for a moment watching, then followed them in black silence.

As the day closed in, they found a small farmhouse

close to the road. There were large, growling dogs in the yard. The man who opened the door looked warily at Koenig, but when he saw the children, he called for his wife and she let them in.

They put Katta down to sleep in the cold, dark loft beneath the rafters of the wooden roof. Smoke from the fire seeped through the dry boards of the floor.

Mathias lay next to her, listening to the sounds of the voices from below and the dogs prowling in the yard outside. He was trying to think what would happen now, but he was almost too tired to care.

He closed his eyes.

Just as sleep took him, he imagined that he heard the creaking wheels of one cart, then another, passing along the road to Felissehaven.

PART TWO
Felissehaven

16
Meiserlann

The harbour was choked with ice. It spread in one solid sheet as far as the small islands where the monastery of St Becca the Old stood. Where the run of the tide had broken it into small rafts, clear water the colour of gun-blued steel showed between the floes. Slack-sailed barges made their way down these channels to the harbour quays, while the big ships that off-loaded onto them rode at anchor as best they could in the cold, heavy swell on the furthest fringes of the ice.

Felissehaven – the city of the smiling angel.

Story had it that an angel had guided St Becca to the offshore islands and, standing in the prow of a small boat, pointed with its feathered wings to the place where the saint should kneel down and pray.

And Becca did. He waded ashore and, while the

angel watched, got down on his bare knees amongst the hard, sharp stones, put his hands together and prayed.

That was a long time ago. They built a monastery there. But now it was nothing but an empty ruin and St Becca just dry bones in a golden reliquary, but the angel lived on – smiling down on the people of Felissehaven from a hundred ornate carvings and the stained glass in their churches. Some people said that the angel had never existed; some that it had never gone away. The only proof of it now were those carvings on the buildings, and the glass in the windows – them, and the image of its face on the city's golden coins and on the Great Seal of the Duke.

Felissehaven.

Buildings with gilded gables and narrow cobbled lanes between. Ornate golden spires that blazed in the cold winter sun. Wide streets and tumbled houses. And on the hill, high above it all, stood the fine palace from which the Duke and his Council looked down on the rich affairs of the buildings squeezed into the city walls beneath them. Looked down on it all and ruled it with a rod of iron.

The day after Katta had the fit, she was slow-witted and confused. Mathias worried for her. He'd never seen anyone like this, not even Gustav when he'd been ill. When she spoke, her words came awkwardly, as though she had to think about each one before she said it. It was painful to watch, so he sat beside her and held her hand in his. It wasn't until the afternoon that she even really understood where she was, and by then it was too late to start. So it was a full day before they set out again. They walked the last dozen miles down into the city, Mathias on the horse and Katta going slowly on foot beside it. Her head hurt her so much. Stefan kept his distance. He walked on the other side of the horse. It was as though each of them were pretending that the other wasn't there. For the moment there was an uneasy quiet between them. At the farmhouse he'd put a bowl of food in front of her and she'd eaten it, which is more than she would have done once. But that didn't mean a thing, Mathias knew. He sat watching them both. It was like a powder keg just waiting for the spark.

Then they had come through the gates and into the city. It was like nothing Mathias had ever seen before. Lutsmann's show had never visited towns like this, with gilded gables and narrow lanes crowded with people and stalls. Even Stefan, who

tried to pretend indifference to it, stared open-mouthed at the things around him. Only Koenig was untouched, and Mathias realized that he must have seen sights like this a hundred times before.

Of the coaching inns inside the city walls, it was one down by the harbour that Koenig chose. The one where the masters of the ships and the merchants of the city met to do their business. He took a room up a flight of narrow stairs. It had one long window that opened out onto the masts of the barges in the harbour – almost close enough to touch them. From there they could see across the ice to the small dark islands and the ships at anchor beyond. For all his travellings, Mathias had never seen a ship.

He sat himself on the window ledge beside Katta, looking out at the sea, his coat collar pulled up to his chin. He had been waiting to speak to her, waiting for her to be herself again, because a thought had been winding quietly away in his head as he sat in the saddle in front of Koenig. He'd wanted to tell her, but there hadn't been a chance until now.

Why would he and Gustav have lived in Lutsmann's cart if Gustav could have simply dug up treasure? That made no sense. That wasn't what Gustav had said anyway. What Gustav had said was that he knew a secret. He didn't say he had one. He *knew* one. And that was different. A secret was something that somebody else didn't want you to know. Maybe that's what the paper showed: where whatever it was – the secret – was hidden.

And that was the thought that was winding in his head. What was it that anyone could want to hide that much?

It was while he was thinking this that he'd remembered something else too, as though the things were somehow tied together. He'd remembered the nights in the cart when Gustav would want to know if the morning was coming yet. Except now he understood that this hadn't been what Gustav had wanted at all. He'd always ask the same thing, staring with wide, mad, eyes – 'Is it lighter?' But it wasn't the morning coming that Gustav had been talking about at all. It had been the man.

Mathias looked up at Katta and his face was pale and serious.

'It's not treasure,' he said. He knew that she wanted it to be, but it wasn't. He glanced over towards Koenig and Stefan, but they weren't looking. He lowered his voice so that Katta had to strain to hear it. 'It's something he knew,' he said.

She wasn't sure that she'd heard him properly – her head was still fuzzy – but then she realized that she had, and she frowned.

'But that ain't worth nothin',' she said.

'It depends what it is,' he answered.

She shook her head, then pulled a face, because it had hurt. 'It's got to be worth something or they wouldn't be tryin' to find it as well.'

Mathias bit his lip and looked at her. This was the other thing he'd thought. 'Who says they are?' he said.

Whatever it was Koenig had in mind, he kept it to himself, though Stefan must have known, because

Koenig sent him out on some errand. He was gone for a couple of hours or so. When he came back, Koenig listened carefully to what he had to say, but it was all in Burner and, try as he might, Mathias couldn't understand a word.

He watched them as they were talking. It was a strange way that Koenig and Stefan had. He couldn't fathom it at all. He'd seen Stefan answer back; other times he'd not answer at all, as though he hadn't heard what Koenig had said, but clearly he had. And when he did that, Koenig would look at him with hard eyes, but he wouldn't do anything. He couldn't imagine anyone else taking that liberty with Koenig. But Stefan did. More's the point, he got away with it. And that puzzled Mathias, because he couldn't see why.

When he'd tried to talk to Katta about it, she hadn't wanted to listen. She'd stopped wondering why Stefan was there – it made sense to her. Koenig would need someone else, like now. Wherever it was that Stefan had gone, Koenig hadn't had to go, and maybe Koenig didn't trust her and Mathias on their own. After the trouble they'd had at the inn, she wasn't sure that she wanted him to. They were safe when he was there in a way they wouldn't be if he wasn't. But whether that would be the same when he found whatever it was they were looking for, she wasn't so sure. For the moment though, she trusted him, which is more than she did Stefan.

The rest of the afternoon slipped past. Come the evening, Koenig told them to get their coats. They were going out.

'Where to?' said Katta.

He looked at her with wry amusement on his face. 'Work it out,' he said.

She didn't think that he'd really meant it, but when he waited for an answer, she realized that he had. Like Mathias, she'd been thinking while they walked – what would she do if she were Koenig? He could go to Dr Leiter and sell the piece of paper, but if he'd been going to do that, he'd have done it already. Leiter was just proof that the paper was worth something. If Koenig wanted to know what it was really worth, he was going to have to find out about it himself.

But how?

There really was only one place she could think of to start. 'Find someone who knew the conjuror,' she said.

Koenig smiled. 'Very good,' he said. 'And who might that be?' He buttoned his thick coat. 'Who might know a conjuror?'

But this time she didn't have an answer. She frowned crossly and looked at Mathias.

'Who might know a conjuror?' Koenig asked him.

For a circus boy, the answer was suddenly blindingly simple.

'Another conjuror,' he said.

Koenig put his hat on his head.

'So where are we goin'?' said Katta.

She still hadn't grasped it. Koenig smiled at her again, his eyes bright with amusement at her confusion.

'To find a conjuror,' he said. 'Or someone who will do just as well.'

There were several theatres in the city. That is where Koenig had sent Stefan – to find out about them. Some were more grand than others. It was one of the lesser ones that Koenig chose, where, he said, they'd be more likely to know the small people as well as the great – the grand theatres wouldn't need to bother with the likes of them.

Katta had never set foot inside a theatre, not even

a shabby theatre like the one she found herself in now. The nearest she'd got were the fairs and travelling shows – like Mathias's – that passed the inn. She held her ticket tight in her hand and stared open-mouthed as the crowd pushed in around her. In the boxes, girls with painted faces waved at the men below. Then, to a cheer, the big candelabras were lit and hoisted up on thick ropes to swing below the rafters of the roof, and the spectacle began. There was a mock fight between a knight and a dragon, which the dragon won, but whether he was supposed to was another matter because they started another fight, a real one, as they left the stage. There was a man who sang and drank at the same time. Then on came a lady who twirled a parasol and did a little skipping dance while she sang, but the crowd didn't like her at all and began whistling and catcalling. She kept at it for as long as she could, then, thumbing her nose, she turned round and, lifting her skirt with a flounce, stuck her bare backside out at them – and then they cheered.

But there was no conjuror.

Katta didn't care; for that moment she'd quite forgotten the world. She stood hooting and cheering with the rest. It was only when, hot-faced and smiling, she turned round and saw Stefan looking at her, the ugly wound across his hard, cold face, that she remembered. She turned quickly to Mathias – and then stopped. He was standing next to her, staring up at the stage. His face was blank and he had tears in his eyes. He could smell the grease-paint. It made him think of the rope around his wrist, of his grandfather dribbling and drunk. Of Anna-Maria and Lutsmann. Of the slaps and beatings; of all the misery that he had endured. She couldn't have known the reason, but she slipped her hand into his, and though he didn't look at her, he took it and held onto it tightly. But the show wasn't the same for her then. It had all been spoiled.

The curtain finally came down, and the crowd began to drift away. But not Koenig. He leaned against a wall and watched the people go until there were none left. Then the curtain was pulled wide again and the stage cleared. An old man began sweeping the floor. He had a small dog at his heel, snapping up what it could find to eat amongst the things that had been dropped.

He'd been sweeping for a while before he noticed them. 'You need to go now,' he said. 'There's no more.'

But Koenig didn't move. He looked up at the roof and into the empty boxes. 'It's many years since I was here,' he said. 'Not much has changed.'

He had judged the old man just right. Ready, given half a chance, to put down his broom and talk.

'When was that?' said the man.

Koenig pulled a thoughtful face, as though trying to reckon when it had been. 'Ten, twelve years. I used to come here often. You were here too – I remember you.'

'I was at the front then,' said the old man wistfully.

Koenig clapped his hands as though he had just recognized a face from the distant past. 'I thought so!' he said.

Katta stared at him. It was so brazen. She almost wondered if he really had been there once. The old man obviously thought he had.

'Times change,' said Koenig.

The man shook his head sadly. 'They do.'

'Who did you have then?' said Koenig, looking for all the world as though he were trying to remember.

'The Great Landee,' said the man.

'Who was . . . ?'

'The fire-eater.'

'Yes!' said Koenig, slapping his hands together

again. 'I remember him. And who else?'

'Lady Juniper.'

'Lady Juniper.' Koenig sighed and put his hand across his heart. 'Not like today, eh?'

'Not like today,' said the man. 'All rubbish. Did you see that woman?'

Koenig shook his head. 'Who was the conjuror?' he said. 'Had a big mark on his face. Name like Hustav? Or Gustav?'

Mathias had been watching it all, waiting for this moment. Now he felt the hairs on the back of his neck creep. He stood very still. But the man looked puzzled. He prodded at the floor with the broom.

'No,' he said at last. 'That was Meiserlann who had the mark on his face. But it wasn't here that you'd have seen him. It was at The Arrow. You must have seen him there. He didn't do here. Too good for us, even then.'

'Is he still about?' said Koenig.

'Meiserlann?' The man shook his head. 'No. He just upped and went, didn't he? Left old Jacob behind, and went.'

Mathias could feel Katta looking at him, but he didn't turn to her. He was staring at the man, waiting for what was going to come next.

205

'Jacob?' said Koenig.

'His dresser. You know – his stage clothes. He's still about though. He drinks at The Bear. I've seen him there. But he's . . .' The man tapped the side of his head with his finger.

'That's sad,' said Koenig. He took a deep breath. 'Well, we must go.'

'I will show you around if you like,' said the man.

'Another time,' said Koenig, and he held out a silver coin. 'Drink on me for old times,' he added.

The man smiled. 'I will,' he said and, taking the coin, dropped it into his coat pocket. Then he began sweeping again with the little dog at his heels.

As they walked away, Mathias didn't know how he felt. It had only ever been 'Mathias' and 'Gustav'. Now, suddenly, there was another name, his name too – Meiserlann. Mathias Meiserlann. He said the names together, and it felt like a door was opening into a past that he knew nothing about. It was his past and it was there to be found.

The Bear was not a difficult place to find, but you wouldn't want to go in unless you had business there. It was in a back alley. There were a few narrow steps leading down to its door. Inside it was dirty and dark. Mathias wasn't even sure if it was open. There was a small stove and a large stuffed bear in one corner. Its fur was worn thin and the innards of shavings and padding poked through the palms of its huge paws. There was no one there. Koenig banged on the counter and called out. Finally a slattern-faced woman with a baby on her hip appeared from a room at the back.

'You want?' she said.

'To find an old friend,' said Koenig.

She looked at him suspiciously, then at the children. Katta did her best to smile, but the woman looked away.

'Old Jacob,' said Koenig. He touched the side of his head so that she might know who he meant. 'He comes here still?'

'He might,' she said.

He put a silver coin under his fingertip and pushed it slowly across the counter towards her. She looked at him and said nothing, so he took another coin and did the same, leaving it just beside the first. For a moment she left them there, as though wondering whether her silence might earn her another, then she realized that it might lose her them both, so she quickly swept each of them up into her apron.

'Later,' she said. 'He comes later.'

'Then we'll wait,' said Koenig.

They sat in the shadows in one corner of the dim room. Men came in ones and twos but the room never filled. They were rough, labouring men, dirty from their day. Few of them spared Koenig more than a glance. Then the door opened and an old man came shuffling in. He was wrapped up against the cold. Koenig was watching the woman behind the counter. Mathias saw her look straight at him and then away, and he knew then that this was Jacob.

Jacob sat at a bench just along the wall from where they were. He wore a heavy coat and scarf, and thick fingerless mittens that he didn't take off. When a pot of beer and a tiny glass of schnapps were brought to him, he used both hands to tip the schnapps into the beer and then to cradle the pot as he lifted it to drink. It seemed to Mathias a very clumsy thing to do.

'Jacob?' said Koenig.

The old man slowly turned his head to see who had said his name.

'It is!' said Koenig. 'Old Jacob – the dresser.'

Jacob looked hard at Koenig and then at the children. 'I don't know you,' he growled, and looked away.

Koenig picked up his drink and went and sat next to Jacob.

'Leave me alone,' said the old man.

'I want to talk to you about the old days,' said Koenig warmly. 'At The Arrow.'

Jacob stared steadily ahead.

'About Meiserlann,' said Koenig.

'I don't know anyone by that name.'

'But you did,' said Koenig. 'You were his dresser.'

Jacob was quiet for a moment. He sat very still. 'I don't know anything,' he said. 'I told them then, and I'll tell you now, I don't know anything.'

'Told who, Jacob?' said Koenig. 'Know what?'

But Jacob cradled his beer and said nothing.

Mathias was staring at the old man's face, trying to remember it. Koenig turned and beckoned to him. Mathias stood up and came over.

'This boy,' said Koenig, 'is Meiserlann's grandson – Mathias.'

Jacob turned his head and looked hard and long at Mathias, then at Koenig. 'Liar,' he said in a quiet, cold voice. 'Meiserlann had no grandson. No wife, no children, no grandson. Only me. Tell you anything?' he sneered.

He took off his mittens and held up his hands in front of Koenig's face. Mathias could see now why he held the pot of beer as he did. He had no thumbs. Only the scars and stumps of where they had once been.

'This is what they did to me,' he said. 'Three days, and I told them nothing. You think I will tell you anything about Meiserlann, Mr Liar?'

He began to put the mittens back on – he had to use his teeth to pull them over his wrist.

'Meiserlann is dead,' said Koenig.

Jacob hesitated for a moment. Then he pulled the last mitten on. 'Liar,' he said.

Standing up, he deliberately turned his back on Koenig and, shuffling to the door, went up the narrow steps and into the dark of the alley outside.

17
Lost and Found

Koenig was on his feet straight away. He spoke quickly in Burner to Stefan. Short, clipped words that Katta knew had to be instructions. Then he turned to her and Mathias.

'Stefan will take you back to the inn,' he said. 'Stay downstairs by the fire, where everybody can see you and you can see everybody else. No one can harm you then. Don't move from there until I come back. Do you understand?'

He looked urgently towards the door, as though even this had wasted too much time. 'I have to see where he goes,' he said. 'It won't be far.'

Before Katta could open her mouth he had turned and gone.

It was the worst thing he could have done – he'd left her alone with Stefan.

When she looked at Stefan, he was staring at her as though not sure what to do with this sudden chance that had fallen into his lap. They both knew what he was thinking, and she wasn't going to let it happen.

She turned to Mathias. 'We could wait here,' she said quickly. 'He won't be long.'

But Mathias wasn't listening. He was still hearing what Jacob had said. The words were going round in his head. *No wife. No children. No grandchildren.*

Katta tugged at his sleeve. 'We could stay here, eh?' she said again. 'What do you think?'

No grandchildren. 'But that can't be right,' he said.

'Course it ain't,' she said. 'It's the wrong man. It must be someone else he's talking about. Come on, we just have to wait here, see?' She was growing more desperate in what she said. 'We'll just wait here. Right?'

She sat down at the bench. But Stefan stood up. He put his arm on Mathias and Mathias turned round and looked at him blankly.

'We go the inn,' said Stefan carefully. 'We do the Koenig says us.'

Then he looked at Katta. 'You do the Koenig says us too.' It sounded like a warning.

'*Tells* us,' said Katta. 'Not *says* us. And we could wait here just as good. You've got another thing coming if you think I'm going with you, Burner boy.'

Stefan had already got his hand on Mathias's arm and began steering him towards the door. Katta sat defiantly where she was, expecting Stefan to stop and argue, but he didn't. He led Mathias through the door and closed it behind them. She watched it for several moments, expecting it to open again, thinking that they would have to come back. But they didn't, and suddenly The Bear didn't seem such a good place to be on her own.

There were fewer people now, and she didn't like the look of them at all. She had seen their sort before. Fleshy-faced, hard-drinking men, with sudden, loud, dirty laughs.

'You on your own now, sweetheart?' said a voice next to her.

She hadn't seen the man step out of the shadows beside the stuffed bear, but he must have been watching her for a while. He put his drinking pot on the table and sat down too close to her. His breath smelled of onions and schnapps.

'I'm waiting for my friend,' she said quickly. 'His name's Koenig. He looks after me.'

'I could look after you just as well, sweetheart,' the man said in a wheedling voice. 'Be a bit of a change for you, wouldn't it?' He pushed his face closer to hers. 'Someone different.'

She tried to stand up but he held onto the sleeve of her coat and pulled her back down.

'Can't go if he's not here yet, can you?' he said, and this time there was a dangerous edge to the words.

'He's just outside,' said Katta.

She snatched her coat out of his hand but, just as quick, he caught hold of it again.

'Maybe we should go and look for him together then?' he said. 'Have a little walk, you and me?'

Still holding onto her with one hand, he drained the pot of beer, then wiped his mouth with the back of the other. 'Let's go and see if he's here yet, shall we?'

He stood up, gripping her arm. She looked about, but there was no one to help as he led her towards the door. He opened it and they went out, up the steps into the dark alley. The ground was frosted and hard with ice. She was praying that Koenig would be there, but he wasn't. The alley was empty.

'Doesn't look like he's here,' the man said, and

pulled her closer to him.

She could feel her heart pounding in her chest. It was now or not at all.

'There he is!' she said.

Startled, the man turned to look, and as he did so, Katta tried to jerk her arm free. She almost managed it, but he had too tight a hold and his fingers closed around the cuff of the coat.

'Oh, no you don't!' he said.

He made a grab at her and she stepped back, but her feet slipped on the ice, and down she went like a stone. But he was still holding on, and her fall pulled him off balance. He lost his footing and down he came as well. But he'd let go. She pushed him away, her feet sliding on the ice. He tried to catch hold of her ankle, but he slipped again and that was enough for Katta. She was on her feet and running as fast as she could keep her balance. She could hear him shouting and swearing at her to come back, but he wasn't chasing her. As she turned the corner, she looked round and saw that he'd fallen again and was lying in the middle of the alley, spread-eagled on his back, but she didn't stop running. She ran until she had no more breath left to run with, and then she stood, bent over, hands on her knees, taking in great lungfuls of air with her heart going bam, bam, bam in her chest.

There was no sign of Stefan or Mathias anywhere. She stood bent over until she'd got her breath back, then walked carefully to the end of the narrow street and looked both ways, but they weren't there. She hadn't a clue where she was. It wasn't that bad, though, she thought. All she had to do was find her way down to the harbour. That would be easy. It might take her some time, but she could do it. If she was lucky, Koenig would already be there and Stefan wouldn't be able to touch her.

She was hot and clammy from running. The air was ice-cold. She pulled up the collar of her coat and, choosing one of the two narrow lanes, began to walk. She went beneath a low arch and came out into a wide paved street.

All along the street, paper lanterns had been strung with candles flickering inside them. Some were decorated with ribbons – blue and white – like the frost that sparkled on them. Others were painted with the face and feathers of a smiling angel. People were strolling together, lots of them. They were all wearing carnival costumes and wrapped in warm cloaks and gowns. Some carried a small feather mask

on a little stick with which to hide their face. Some had whole masks – she could see Pierrot faces, animals and beaked birds. The people bowed to each other as they passed. She could hear singing and laughing. In the middle of the street, big fiery braziers had been lit, and men were selling hot chestnuts, pastries and wine. She stood staring. It looked like a dream. For a moment she thought it was.

Along the edges of the street, their backs against the buildings, children stood and watched. When she looked up at the windows, she saw that there were other children leaning out of them too. She began to walk open-mouthed, staring at the costumes and the people as they strolled on each side of her.

When she came to a group of children standing in a doorway, she stopped.

'What's this all about?' she said.

They looked at her as though they thought the whole world would know.

'It's the Festival of the Angel tomorrow,' a boy said.

She turned round and looked down the street. 'This happen every year?' she said.

The boy laughed at her. 'You stupid?' he said.

'I'm not from here,' she answered.

'Yeah,' he said. 'Tomorrow's church day. You not seen it then?'

'No,' she said.

She stood staring at the fires and the lanterns. 'It's wonderful.'

The boy nodded knowingly at his friends. 'You want to go up the other end,' he said. 'It's better up there. You can see them all coming out the opera.' He pointed. 'It's right down there,' he said. 'That's where you want.'

A woman in a fine gown swept past, and then Katta found out why the children were standing, waiting. Why they were so keen to send her on her way.

'Sweets, lady!' they all cried at once, holding their hands out towards her.

The woman lifted the little mask she carried to her face and, putting her hand into the folds of her cloak, scattered something on the ground at their feet. At once the children forgot Katta and were scrabbling and fighting in the frost for the sweets that had been strewn for them. There was a chorus of voices from the open windows above.

'Sweets, lady!'

But she had already passed on, leaving the squabbling children behind her.

Katta didn't try to pick up any of the sweets: she knew there'd be a fight if she did. So she turned her back on them and looked down the street.

There was plenty of time, she thought. She didn't need to find her way back just yet. If she was late, there'd be more chance that Koenig would be there, and he'd be more angry with Stefan for leaving her behind. The thought of that made her smile.

No. There was still time yet.

She began to walk slowly along the wide street, the way the boy had pointed. She wanted to see the fine people coming out of the opera. As she walked, she watched the ladies, saw how they nodded their heads to each other, how the men made graceful bows, and she tried to make herself taller and walk like them. There was a bright green-and-gold feather on the ground that had fallen from a mask. Picking it up, she brushed it against her cheek and walked on, pretending that she was a fine lady and that the feather was a mask of her own.

Trinket stalls and booths lined the street. People were selling whistles and ribbons, brooches and pins. In one place a small crowd had gathered in front of a painted cart, and Katta pushed her way forward, the better to see what it was they were watching. One side of the cart had been opened to make a small stage. Tar flares were burning in front of it. A fat moustached man in a ringmaster's coat was beating on a big drum while a thin woman in a tight silk costume doubled and folded her body through tiny hoops, as though she were a snake. People were throwing money – coins that glinted in the light of the flares – but Katta had nothing to throw. She watched for a while, then wandered on.

A much larger crowd had gathered in front of the big white building at the end of the street. As before, Katta pushed and wormed her way to the front of it. Wide stone steps led up to the open doors of a grand entrance. Footmen in velvet coats and powdered wigs stood beside the doors while people in carnival costume made their way down the steps in ones and twos to the waiting carriages. The ladies wore jewels that sparkled as they went by.

Then two men came down the steps together. One was very tall. He wore the red and purple robes of a churchman, but even he held a small mask in his hand. He was talking to the man beside him; he'd taken his mask off too – it hung loosely by its ribbons from his fingers. Katta saw the mask first and only then the face – and her heart stopped. She'd seen that face before. She pushed herself back into the crowd as the man passed by, but he didn't notice her, which was just as well, because his face was round like a moon, and in the hand that didn't hold the mask he carried a silver-topped cane.

Stefan and Mathias had walked most of the way back to the inn before Mathias really understood that Katta wasn't with them. The whole time he had been thinking about what Jacob had said and what it must mean.

If the man at the theatre had been right, then the conjuror with the mark on his face was Meiserlann. Unless there had been two – but you wouldn't get two people, not two conjurors, the same, with a big stain like that on their face. It was the thing that Gustav had always kept hidden. It was what Leiter had looked for first – why he'd washed the white paint from Gustav's face. It had to be – Meiserlann was Gustav.

But Meiserlann had no wife, no children. Jacob would know a thing like that. He wouldn't have to lie about it, and it could mean only one thing. Mathias could hardly bear to say it.

'He wasn't my grandfather,' he said. 'He never was.'

It had been the one thing that had made him stay. All those times he would have run away but for that one fact, and it hadn't been true.

Ever.

He felt suddenly sick. He looked about for Katta, but she wasn't there. The street was empty.

'Where's Katta?' he said.

Stefan kept on walking. Mathias caught him by the arm and stopped him.

'Where's Katta?'

'We go the inn,' said Stefan. 'The Koenig says us.'

'But we've left her behind.'

'The Koenig says us,' said Stefan coldly, and he pushed Mathias's hand away. 'We go the inn.'

'Not without Katta,' said Mathias. He began to walk back the way they had come, but Stefan grabbed him by his arm and pulled him back. Mathias winced.

'We go the inn,' said Stefan.

He didn't let go of Mathias's arm.

Suddenly, in the street behind them, came the sound of firecrackers – several, all at once. Instinctively they turned to see what it was, and as they did so, a crowd of youths and boys came running and dancing round the corner. They had fireworks on sticks and were waving them in the air. Showers of silver and gold sparks fell all around them. Each one wore a black mask in the shape of a big beaked bird. Some had them pushed up onto the top of their heads, others down over their faces. They were blowing horns and beating drums. A huge banner of an angel in a boat flew above them as they ran, whooping and shouting. They were upon Mathias and Stefan before they had realized what was happening.

Grabbing hold of them, they pushed the two boys from one to another, then, tripping them, they sat on them and smeared their clothes and hair with thick treacle from a pot and covered them with cold ashes from a sack. Stefan was the first to scramble to his feet; with his arms covering his head, he turned and ran. He could hear whistles and jeers behind him, but he didn't stop. He ran until, breathless, he found himself at the end of a narrow street with a lantern burning above it. He pushed himself into the safe dark of a doorway and stood there, shaking. He could hear the sound of the firecrackers and drums growing fainter in the distance. He waited until he couldn't hear them at all, then, slowly, he poked his head round the doorway. With a rising sense of panic he looked back down the street. It was completely empty.

Mathias had gone.

Mathias hadn't been able to run. He'd lain where he was on the ground while the boys had kicked him and dropped firecrackers around him. Then someone had thought of claiming him as their prize. They'd picked him up like a sack and, hoisting him above their heads, they'd run laughing and whooping headlong down the street, blowing horns and beating their drums, sparks and f..e-crackers raining around them, the banner fluttering over their heads. Mathias had cried out in pain with each agonizing jolt, but they paid no heed. A huge screaming wheel of light was going round and round in his head, but they just ran and ran.

They carried him up and down, running bedlam through the crowds, until at last they'd had enough of him. They dropped him in a back alley, making mocking bows in front of him as though he were a god. Then, with a last kick, hooting and laughing, they were gone. He could hear the drums and the horns getting fainter and fainter, then all was quiet. He lay on his back and closed his eyes.

He didn't know how long he lay there like that, but it must have been for a long time. When finally he opened his eyes again, there was a rime of frost in his hair and he was shaking with the cold. The screaming light in his head had stopped; there was just inky silence. He lay on his back, looking up at the line of black sky marking the narrow gap between the dark tall buildings that reached over him.

Slowly he crawled onto his hands and knees. He'd been left in the dirty gutter of a narrow street. He said Stefan's name, but Stefan was nowhere to be seen. He pulled himself to his feet and found that he was leaning against the side of a cart. He was covered from head to foot in ash and treacle. He stood swaying unsteadily, with his eyes closed and his arms hugging his ribs. They hurt so much. He could hardly breathe. He wasn't sure he could walk at all.

Then he realized that he could hear noises. They were coming from the cart. Someone was moving about inside. He opened his eyes. The street was quite dark. The only light came from the cart itself – just a thin crack through one of its shutters. He stood, listening. Maybe whoever it was would help him if he asked. Very slowly, he made his way round the cart until he found its steps. They were very steep. He stood holding the rail while a wave of pain swept over him. Then he took a teaspoon of breath and, one by one, he went up the steps and tapped on the dark door. The sounds inside stopped but nothing happened, so he tapped again.

This time there were different noises – a bolt being slid back, and then another, and the door opened just a crack, spilling warm, yellow lamplight into the street. Mathias lifted his face and was about to speak but the words died in his mouth.

Standing in the doorway, face painted, lips as dark as blood, was Anna-Maria.

She didn't recognize him at once, this ash-covered boy in a Burner's coat. He could see that she hadn't and, mumbling an apology, he began to back slowly down the steps, and that was his mistake. Anna-Maria might not have recognized him, but she knew his voice. He saw her eyes suddenly widen as she realized who he was. He tried to turn round but she shot out her hand and grabbed hold of his coat.

'Lutsmann!' she shouted.

He tried to push her hand away, but the ends of bones grated in his chest and he folded like a broken toy. It was all she needed. She caught hold of him with both hands and, pulling him off his feet, dragged him by his collar up the last of the steps and into the cart, kicking the door shut behind her with her pointed shoe.

The light seemed so bright. Lutsmann was lying on the small cot bed in his shirt and braces. He stared with drink-bleary eyes, first at his wife and then at Mathias. Anna-Maria pushed Mathias forward with her foot.

'Look who I've found,' she said.

18
Things Told

The old man was already at the end of the alley, but Koenig could see him well enough – a dark shadow moving against the darker shadows of the buildings. He wasn't walking quickly. Koenig let him go a few paces more and then followed.

It was as he had thought – Jacob had not come far. The old man walked over a small bridge, then into a narrow alley with tall uneven buildings reaching across on both sides, almost blocking out the dark sky above. A gutter piled high with frozen filth ran down the middle of it. On both sides, all the way along, there were slits of light showing through the cracks of closed shutters. Somewhere a dog was barking. Jacob did not once look round. He walked steadily to the end of the alley, where an open doorway led into one of the shabby buildings. A candle stub was burning just inside, and by the light of it Koenig saw him slowly climbing the wooden stairs.

Koenig quickened his pace; coming to the foot of the stairs, he stood, hand on the banister, listening, counting Jacob's shuffling steps until they stopped. There was the sound of keys and a door opened and shut. Koenig waited a moment, listening to the noises from the other rooms above, but there were no more steps. Quietly, keeping count, he began to climb the stairs.

When he had counted the right number, he came to a landing with two doors opening from it. He listened at the first. He could hear the sound of a man and a woman talking inside. Then the woman laughed. He moved across the landing and put his ear to the other door and there was silence. As he touched the door, it moved. It hadn't been properly shut. He pushed it with one finger and it swung slowly open. The room inside was in complete darkness. It smelled stale and damp.

'One step, Mr Liar,' said a voice from the dark, 'and I'll blow your brains out.'

Koenig didn't move. He couldn't work out where the old man was – whether he was near enough for him to reach before he had time to pull the trigger – so he stood quite still.

'I want to speak with you, Jacob,' he said.

'You can say what you like from where you are,' came the answer.

He had where the man was now. He was in the furthest corner of the room. It was too far to reach.

'The boy really believes that Meiserlann was his grandfather,' said Koenig.

'Liar.'

'I did not say it was true. I said it is what he believes. He knew him by another name – Gustav.'

There was a long silence.

'Are you still there, Jacob?' said Koenig.

'Go on,' said the old man.

'Meiserlann died. Sewn into his coat was a piece of paper – half a piece of paper. The boy found it. People have tried to kill him to get it. I want to know why.'

There was another long silence, then the sound of movement and a flint being struck on a tinderbox. A flame flared. Jacob had lit a lamp.

'Come in, Mr Liar,' he said.

The room was squalid and small. There was a filthy bed, and an unlit stove. Jacob, wrapped in his coat, sat in a chair with a pistol cradled awkwardly between his thumbless hands.

'You live alone here?' said Koenig.

The old man looked around at the dirty room. 'You call this living?' he said.

Koenig shook his head. 'No.'

Jacob lifted the pistol a little so that it pointed at Koenig's heart. 'There was a fat man,' he said. 'He came to the theatre just to watch Meiserlann. He sat in the very best box. He would buy Meiserlann meals and give him presents. He never knew how Meiserlann laughed about him behind his back – at his little handkerchief and his perfumed shirts. He was Meiserlann's very own private joke. You know what his name was?'

'No,' said Koenig.

'Gustav. How did you come by that name, Mr Liar?'

Slowly Koenig held his two hands up, palms out to show Jacob that he had nothing in them. Then, one hand still held like that, he reached slowly into his coat with the other and drew out his flat leather wallet. He opened it and held up the piece of paper for Jacob to see.

'What I want to know is why this is worth so much, Jacob.'

'It is worth nothing, Mr Liar,' said the old man, and then he smiled, a crooked, clever smile. 'Unless you know where the other piece is.'

'How much would it be worth then?'

Jacob shrugged. 'It might just be enough to save your life,' he said. He shifted his grip on the pistol. 'Meiserlann said he would come back. I believed him. I was more afraid of losing him than I was of losing my thumbs. So I said nothing, even when they cut them off. Now you tell me he is dead. Who are you to know, Mr Liar?'

'I found the boy.'

'Then let him tell me himself,' said Jacob. 'Because I don't believe you.'

Koenig slipped the piece of paper back into his wallet. 'Where shall I bring him?' he said.

'Here,' said Jacob. 'Bring him here. Then we shall see.'

Anna-Maria and Lutsmann sat staring at Mathias. It was too good to be true, like finding a solid gold watch in a ditch. Anna-Maria had taken the precaution of tying his wrists with a thin, biting rope, one end of which she'd fastened to a hook in the roof, higher than he could hope to reach. But she needn't have bothered. Mathias didn't have the strength to do anything. He lay in a crumpled heap on the floor.

'So,' said Anna-Maria. 'You ran away, after all the trouble we took for you. You ungrateful little scab!' She slapped his head.

'Let the boy speak, my plum,' said Lutsmann in a false, brandy-fumed voice. 'Didn't he come back to us all on his own? He must have wanted to tell us something very much.'

'The only thing I want him to tell us,' hissed Anna-Maria, and she put her face close to Mathias's – so close that he could smell the perfumed powder, the peppermint breath, 'is what Leiter wanted to know.'

Mathias closed his eyes; his head drooped on his shoulders. 'I don't know,' he said in a whisper.

'I don't believe you,' said Anna-Maria in a voice silky quiet and full of menace. 'I don't think you are telling me the truth.'

'I am,' said Mathias. But he couldn't look at her.

'Do you know what I do to filthy, dirty, lying little boys who don't tell me the truth? I do this.'

She put the heel of her hand on Mathias's broken chest and leaned all her weight down on it. The pain was unbearable. Mathias let out a long broken cry. Anna-Maria sat back and watched him.

Lutsmann went quite white. 'P-p-people will hear,' he said.

'Let them,' said Anna-Maria.

'But—'

'Go outside if you haven't the stomach for it,' she snapped. 'If anyone comes, tell them we have the barber here, pulling the boy's bad tooth.'

She looked back down at Mathias, who was doubled up with pain. 'I don't think it will take us that long.'

She leaned forward and, with gritted teeth, pushed even harder.

Lutsmann stood outside in the dark street with his

coat wrapped around him and his fingers stuffed in his ears. Every now and then he would take them out just a little to see if it was all over yet, but then there would be another long scream and he would quickly jam them back in. But no one heard. No one came. And while he stood there, over the roofline of the town, fireworks began to burst in great flowering balloons. Fingers stuffed in his ears, he tipped his fat face up to the sky and watched them.

Then Anna-Maria came out. She came down the steps and stood beside him in her thick coat with its high fur collar. Looping her arm comfortably through his, she smiled at him, and they stood like that, side by side, and watched the fireworks together.

Anna-Maria had found out everything. She knew about the piece of paper and Katta. She knew about Koenig and Jacob. She knew it all.

The question now was, what was she going to do with what she had found out?

19

Anna-Maria and Lutsmann Pay a Visit

The day of the Feast of the Angel dawned ice cold. There was not a breath of wind, not a cloud in the sky. Bells rang out over the waking city – clamorous and discordant. With each passing minute more were joined until the air was thick with the noise of them. There wasn't one corner of a room, not one bucket in a yard, that the sound didn't fill.

Katta hadn't slept. She'd watched the day come in slow creeping light, heard the very first bells ring. Now, that seemed hours ago. She pushed at the food, steaming hot in the bowl, but she couldn't eat it.

The night before, Koenig had arrived back at the inn to find only Stefan by the fire. Katta had followed, almost on his heels, ready to enjoy what happened next. But it didn't happen.

There was no Mathias.

They'd gone straight back into the streets, Koenig carrying a burning tar flare to light their way – but where were they to start? Everywhere they went was crowded with carnival-masked men and feather-faced women. They looked down into the empty dark alleys where the revellers wouldn't go. But Mathias was nowhere to be found. As they searched the streets, the sky above them filled with bursting fireworks. Then even the fireworks were over, and one by one the people drifted away until the streets were bare, but still they hadn't found him. Finally they had to accept that there was nothing to do but go back to the inn and start again in the morning. There was always the chance that Mathias had found his way there and would be waiting for them. But he wasn't.

Then had come the recriminations.

Now they sat silent over their bowls of food.

'We will start where we were last night,' said Koenig. 'I will go one way and you two will go the other.'

Katta couldn't even begin to say what was in Koenig's mind. Whether it was that he'd needed to take Mathias to Jacob and they'd lost him, or whether it was the harm that might have befallen the boy. She wasn't even going to try to guess. She felt sick. If she hadn't stayed in The Bear, none of it would have happened.

She glanced up at Stefan. Koenig caught her do it and, as though reading her thoughts, lifted a warning finger in front of her face.

'This time, you stay with him,' he said. 'This time, you will do as you are told.'

She hadn't ever seen him look more dangerous. It was not a time to argue.

'So long as he don't hurt me,' she said. 'Tell him he can't hurt me. Tell him so as he knows. Say he can't touch me.'

For a moment Koenig said nothing. Then he turned to Stefan. '*Ne tzima loy,*' he said. '*Dash jah?*'

Stefan looked up at her; even he wasn't going to risk a wrong word now. He nodded. '*Dash jah.*'

But he said it as though it was a very hard thing to be asked not to do. '*Ne tzima loy.*'

Anna-Maria and Lutsmann sat waiting in a fine marble hall. Lutsmann was staring around at the gilded ornaments and furniture with his mouth open and his eyes popping wide. Anna-Maria, momentarily disconcerted, sat very still beside him. It was not what they had expected at all.

When they'd set out, leaving Mathias tied and gagged in the cart, they'd expected to find Dr Leiter in a small house in the town. Something with a brass bell pull, a few stone steps up to a polished door – but not this. They sat uneasily, looking about them at the colonnaded pillars and the paintings on the ceiling and walls. But it was where Leiter had said that word was to be sent to him. They'd asked the way, so there was no mistaking it.

As they'd come up through the town, the bells had been ringing and the streets were almost empty. The few people already about were church-dressed and sombre-faced. The day of the Feast of the Angel was a much more serious affair than the mayhem that had gone on the night before. They'd made their way through the lower streets and up to the fine buildings at the top of the hill, where the Duke's palace stood and the great church of the Angel of Felissehaven watched over everything below.

Once admitted, they'd been left in the marble hall to wait for whatever was going to happen next. They could still hear the bells ringing outside. The morning light flooded in through great high

239

windows, making the gold more golden and the paintings more brilliant.

'Are we sure this is the right place?' said Lutsmann uncertainly.

Before Anna-Maria had the chance to tell him that he was a fool, a door at the end of the hall opened and a man came through. But it wasn't Dr Leiter. It was merely someone to take them to him. They followed the man across the marble floor and up a wide staircase. Portraits of stern-faced men looked down on them. A large chandelier hung at the end of a gilded chain, and suddenly Anna-Maria didn't feel quite so certain of herself as she had been. Not as certain as she'd been in the cart when she'd finished with Mathias and first thought of what they were going to do next. This was all much more grand than she'd expected. But she told herself that she'd met Leiter before. She'd dealt with him then, and she'd deal with him again. But all the same, she was uneasy. Only powerful people lived in houses like this, and powerful people were dangerous.

The man stopped at a door. He tapped on it and, without waiting for a reply, opened it and ushered Anna-Maria and Lutsmann inside. Then he made a small bow and, withdrawing, closed the door behind him.

The room was as magnificent as anything they'd already seen. Dr Leiter was sitting at a large table in the middle of it, his fingers steepled to his lips. He had been interrupted in his morning affairs. He had church to attend. Then the procession of the Duke. But this was important.

He watched them come in. He didn't say anything until the door had shut.

'What brings you here, circus man?' he said.

Anna-Maria began to sob. She dabbed at her eyes with her handkerchief. 'It's the boy,' she breathed. 'What has become of the poor boy?'

Leiter's face might have been carved from stone – its expression gave nothing away. 'Why do you need to know?' he said.

What Anna-Maria wanted to know was why the piece of paper was so important, and in that she had a start on Leiter. She had the boy. But she wasn't going to let him know that.

With great difficulty, she controlled her tears a little. Lutsmann guided her to a chair and she sat down.

'We heard that he was lost – the lamb,' she sniffed.

241

'We thought that we might be able to help you find him – he is like our own son. We know little things about him that might be of use to you in looking.'

Leiter's expression did not change. 'Like what?' he said coldly.

'Oh, his little ways.' She dabbed at her eyes again. 'Little things he told us about Gustav.' She watched Leiter through the lace of the hanky as she said the name. 'Just little things.'

Lutsmann put a comforting arm about her shoulder. He knew what was required of him.

'Little things,' said Leiter to himself. 'I wonder how little?'

There was a worn green leather box on the table beside him. He undid the brass clasp, opened it, and set Marguerite down in front of him. She turned her pretty head and looked up at him as he laid out the two cards, first the blue one, then the red.

Mathias had told Anna-Maria many things – she'd made sure of that. But she hadn't quite made sure enough. Small details had slipped by her.

Marguerite was one of them.

Anna-Maria looked at the doll and then at Lutsmann. 'Ah-ha, ah-ha,' she sobbed, and dabbed the hanky to her eyes again.

'Why are you here?' said Leiter.

'Oh, Doctor Leiter,' gasped Anna-Maria, 'we just want to help.'

Marguerite touched the red card.

'You don't happen to know where the boy is, do you?' said Leiter.

'Oh, that we did!' said Anna-Maria, looking up at Lutsmann's face and grasping at his hand for support. He patted her reassuringly. 'We have not seen him since that sad parting.'

Marguerite touched the red card.

'How sad for you,' said Leiter. 'Did you know that the wretched boy took something that was not his before he ran off?'

Anna-Maria's painted face became a picture of shamed outrage. 'Oh – oh! The scoundrel!'

'I want it back,' said Leiter coldly. 'You wouldn't know where it is, would you?'

'How could we?'

Marguerite touched the red card.

Leiter leaned forward. There was a small silver bell upon the table. He rang it and sat back. The door opened and the man who had brought them up the stairs came in. He made a small bow.

'Has my servant returned yet?' said Leiter.

244

'Yes, Doctor Leiter,' said the man.

'Have him come to me.'

The man bowed again and closed the door.

'How may we be of help?' said Anna-Maria. She wanted to move the matter along more to her liking.

But Leiter didn't answer. He pushed back his chair and walked to the window. From it he could see the roofs of the town laid out like patchwork below him; the narrow roads, the glittering ice in the harbour, the islands beyond. The bells were ringing in the cold, clean air.

'Sometimes people make mistakes,' he said. 'They pretend that something is true, when it isn't true at all. Like you have just done.'

Anna-Maria looked up at Lutsmann.

'I assure you, good sir—' Lutsmann began, but he didn't finish whatever it was he was going to say.

In the panelled wall behind Leiter, a door opened and a barrel-squat figure, smaller than a man, larger than a child, stepped into the room.

'If you tell me the truth now,' said Leiter. 'No harm will come to you. You have my word.'

Behind him, on the table, Marguerite smiled her prettiest, sharp-toothed smile and touched the red card.

The gag dug tightly into the corners of Mathias's mouth. Anna-Maria had wanted to be certain that he wouldn't make a sound. She'd tied his wrists and ankles and pushed him into a corner of the cart behind the cot bed; next, she'd covered him with the rag rug that was spread on the floor, pushing a chair against it all so that he couldn't be seen. Then she'd painted her face – lips dark as blood – put on her best cloak and, making sure that Lutsmann was ready, set off to find Leiter.

But someone had watched them go.

Estella had had enough of Lutsmann and Anna-Maria. That slap around the face the night Gustav died had been the last straw. She'd decided that she would take her things and go. She'd just needed the right place and the right time.

Felissehaven was both.

She'd gathered together the few things that belonged to her, and then thought to take a few that belonged to Lutsmann – or, better still, to Anna-Maria. It seemed only right.

She'd thought that she would have to choose a moment when their backs were turned. She couldn't believe her luck when she saw Anna-Maria painted to the nines and Lutsmann in his shining black ring-master's boots lock the door and come down the steps of the cart. Anna-Maria slipped her arm through Lutsmann's, and off they went together. Estella watched for several moments, but they didn't come back.

The lock on the door wasn't enough to stop her. She knew that, slung beneath the cart in a box, were the various tools they used to set up the stage. She opened it and took out a long sharp chisel, which she jammed between the door and the frame, working it from side to side it until the lock gave way. Then she slipped through the door, closed it behind her and looked about.

Lutsmann had a pull-down shelf against one side of the cart. It served as his writing slope and desk. It was where they all came to be paid – when they *were* paid, that is. Behind it there were small drawers stuffed with papers and bills. One by one Estella pulled each of them out and tipped it onto the floor, but there was nothing worth taking. She ran her hand along the shelves where the plates and cups were stored. Then she took the lid from the teapot and shook it upside down, but it was empty, so she dropped that too. There had to be something somewhere. She turned round and looked at the cot bed.

Maybe beneath the mattress?

She pulled the covers and sheets from it – and then stopped still, listening. There'd been a noise. It had come from the corner. It was only then that she noticed the chair and the rug. They looked out of place. Instinctively she looked at the floor where the rug should be, and then back to where the noise had come from.

Curious now, she moved the chair and pulled the rug away.

At first she didn't understand what it was that she was seeing. Mathias was squeezed into the dark corner with his back to her and his face to the wall. His coat, all covered in ash and treacle, might have been a dirty old blanket. It was all she could see of him. She tugged at it and only then realized that it was a child. Reaching down, she put her finger under its chin and, hooking the face up towards her, saw who it was.

'Well, well,' she said. 'What have we here?'

She took a sharp knife from one of the drawers and, none too carefully, cut the rope that tied the gag, so that Mathias could speak. He barely had the strength to say anything.

'Help me,' he said quietly. 'Please help me?'

Estella stood looking at him like a lizard might look at a fly. Then she leaned her face nearer to his, and in that cat-silk voice of hers said, 'Now, why should I want to do that?'

20
Estella

Mathias couldn't turn his head enough to see what Estella was doing next. He could hear her moving around in the cart but could only guess what it was by the sounds she was making as she pulled the last covers from the bed and heaved the mattress onto the floor. That was where she'd found Lutsmann and Anna-Maria's money, locked in a metal box, stuffed at the bottom of the mattress. At least, it sounded like money when she shook it, and that was good enough for her. She took the chisel she'd used on the door and prised the lid open. Mathias heard the scraping of metal on metal and the loose shower of coins cascading onto the wooden floor as the lid suddenly flew open. She swept them up and then Mathias heard her leave – the sound of her feet going down the steps outside. But something made her stop, because she came quickly back up into the cart again. He tried to turn his head.

'Please?' he said.

She pushed the bottom of the bed out of the way and, stepping into the gap she'd made, bent over him. Gripping her fingers in his hair, she pulled his face round towards her. In her hand was the knife she'd used to cut the gag.

'You'd tell, wouldn't you, pretty boy?' she hissed. 'You'd say who'd been here, wouldn't you? Save your own dirty little neck.'

Suddenly he was very frightened, because he knew what she was going to do next. 'No,' he said, and his voice was fluttering like a bird. 'I wouldn't tell.'

'But you would if they made you. Then there'd be a rope waiting for my neck if they ever caught up with me.' She wound her fingers tighter, the edge of the blade brushing against his face.

'No,' said Mathias quickly. 'I wouldn't tell on you.'

'But I can't be sure of that, can I? And we've always been such – good – friends.' She gritted her teeth and pulled hard on his hair as she said each word.

'Yes,' he said, but it was no more than a whisper.

She pulled his hair even tighter.

'Yes!'

'So I'm going to help you,' she said in a quick, vicious voice. 'That's what friends do, isn't it? They help each other.'

'Yes.'

'Then they'll think it was you took their money. And it will be your neck they put the rope around if they catch up with you, not mine.'

Momentarily she held the knife in front of his eyes, then she slit through the cords around his wrists and ankles, picked up the box and went through the door. On the top step she turned round and looked back at him.

'You'd better be quick,' she said. 'Or they might – just – come – back.'

He heard the sound of her feet going down the steps, and this time she didn't stop.

Anna-Maria had shoved him as far into the corner as she could get him, and the cords had been tied very tight. As the blood came slowly back to Mathias's hands and feet, it felt as though they were on fire. He couldn't move without hurting. Slowly he unwound himself until he lay on his back, looking up into the roof of the cart. But there was no time to rest. Estella was right. They might come back at any moment. If he went, they'd be sure to think it was he who'd stolen the money. But if he stayed? This was the only chance he was going to get. He pulled himself to his feet and the cart swam giddily around him. Reaching out with one hand, he leaned on the door frame to steady himself. Then, squinting against the bright morning sun, he went down the steps like an old man.

Stefan had given his word to Koenig that he wouldn't hurt Katta. But keeping his word wasn't something that Stefan was very good at doing. If you knew him, it wasn't something that you'd really want to have to rely on.

Here she was, and here was his chance.

It would be easy to do. There were enough dark alleys. He could say he'd lost her – but he knew Koenig wouldn't believe that. And he'd still have to find Mathias.

Or maybe, if he found Mathias, he could lose Katta.

As though she could hear what he was thinking, Katta kept her distance from him. She wouldn't let him walk behind her. She made sure that she knew where he was. Sometimes he'd go down a side alley and motion for her to follow him, but she wouldn't.

She'd wait, letting him look down there on his own. He always came back too quickly for her liking, and then she wasn't sure that he'd really been looking at all.

But he was, because that's what he'd decided to do.

He was going to find Mathias, and then he'd settle his account with this girl who'd pulled a knife across his good-looking face, even if it meant breaking his word to Koenig. He'd just need to be careful how he did it.

Besides, he'd broken his word to Koenig before. He'd had a lot of practice doing it. The reason was the thing that Mathias had seen but hadn't been able to understand – the way that Stefan got away with so much. The answer was very simple.

He was Koenig's brother.

That was why he'd come with them. It was his last chance to show Koenig what he could do. It wasn't easy living in the shadow of someone like Koenig. Koenig who rode the big horse. Koenig who was everything Stefan wasn't. Koenig who could fight. Koenig who was never scared. Koenig who everyone liked or, if not, respected.

It was like living under a mountain, and the sun never shone on Stefan.

But this was his chance. And what had he done? He'd fallen asleep when he'd been left to stay awake. He'd lost the boy because he'd run away – Koenig knew that. Of course he knew it.

But in Stefan's mind, none of it was his fault. There was only one person to blame.

Katta.

It wasn't just the knife, though that would have been enough. It was everything else too.

All morning they walked the streets of the lower town while the church bells rang. At first Katta would stop people and ask them if they'd seen a boy, but most – if they stopped at all – just shrugged. One street boy looked like another. In the end she gave up even asking. She looked in doorways and behind the filth piled beside the road, but it was hopeless. He was nowhere to be seen.

Then Stefan had given a shout and started running. Katta had run too, her heart racing, but the boy he'd seen wasn't Mathias. They realized it as soon as he turned his head and stared at them, and then it felt even worse.

At last there was nothing to do but go back to the inn and wait for Koenig. See if he'd had any better luck. So they began to walk back down the hill towards the harbour.

As they did so, Katta stopped to look at the ice and the islands beyond.

She hardly noticed the boy huddled in the dark doorway until he moved.

It was Mathias.

As Katta bent over him, he flinched away. He thought that she was Anna-Maria come to find him. She had to hold onto him and say her name over and over again until at last he heard her and understood who she really was.

All the time she was bent over him, Stefan stood behind her, looking up and down the street, his hand holding something inside his coat. But there were too many people. By the time Katta turned round and looked up at him, he'd taken his hand out of his coat, and she never knew what he'd been about to do.

Between them, Stefan and Katta carried Mathias back to the inn. Koenig wasn't there. They laid Mathias on the bed. Katta sat beside him, holding his hand, but he didn't speak. There was so much that he had to tell Koenig, and he was saving his strength for that. But when Koenig came, he wouldn't listen. He tipped a whole cupful of the dark drink into Mathias's mouth, and before Mathias could say anything, the soft hooked feathers of sleep began to fill his head. He wanted to tell about Anna-Maria – that she knew everything. He wanted to say who it was she and Lutsmann had gone to see, but the words wouldn't come. His tongue was fat and filled his whole head. It wouldn't move. If he shut his eyes, he thought, maybe he could open them and try again. But his eyelids were so heavy.

So heavy.

Valter stood in Lutsmann's cart. He had broken all Lutsmann's fingers, one by one. Bent them back until they'd snapped like dry sticks. Lutsmann had told him where the boy was straight away. But Valter had still broken all his fingers just the same. It had been a good game. It had made up for losing the boy in the wood and walking empty-handed all the way back.

But there was no sign of the boy here.

The cut cords that Anna-Maria had tied Mathias with lay on the floor. Valter picked them up and sniffed at them. They smelled of the boy, but they were cold to the touch. He'd been gone a long time. For a moment he stood looking around at the cart. It was all awry. He could see that someone had searched it, but didn't know what it meant. Then he noticed something smeared on the door frame. He tipped his head to one side and looked at it. Touching it, he put his fingers to his mouth and licked them. Whatever it was smelled of the boy, but tasted of ash and treacle. He stood at the top of the steps and looked out. Sharp though his sense of smell was, Valter couldn't follow Mathias's scent through the town; there were too many other stinks that overlaid it.

He curled the cut cords around his hand and slipped them into his pocket. His master hadn't let him ask the woman any questions yet. There hadn't been time for that. Maybe, if he did, thought Valter, she would know where the boy had gone.

He smiled – a slow, cruel smile.

He knew lots of games they could play to help her remember.

While Mathias slept, Koenig had taken his coat and shirt from him and dressed his shoulder as best he could. Then he had bound Mathias's ribs tight. But Mathias was ill. That was obvious. There was a grey pallor to his skin that hadn't been there before. When Koenig put his hand to the boy's head, it was hot and waxy to the touch. He needed a doctor, not a drug.

Katta could see that too. She'd watched Koenig clean Mathias's shoulder and make a pad of Tashka's paste, then wrap the wounds again and tighten the bandage around his chest. But it wasn't care, she told herself. It was just keeping Mathias alive – that's all Koenig wanted. He needed Mathias if he was going to find the other piece of paper. Then what would he do? He didn't need her at all. He only needed Mathias. She felt the palms of her hands grow damp. She could go downstairs now and slip away – it wouldn't matter. He probably wouldn't even come after her. But she'd been there before, and she couldn't do it. She looked at Mathias, waxen-faced on the bed, and knew that she couldn't leave him on his own.

'He needs to see a doctor,' she said.

'After we have seen Jacob,' said Koenig. 'We will take him then.'

'No,' said Katta. 'He needs a doctor now.'

'Tonight,' said Koenig, and he wasn't going to be moved. 'After we have seen Jacob.'

There was no choice.

'He's got to see a doctor then,' she said.

'He will,' said Koenig.

But she didn't believe him.

The rest of the day crept past while Mathias slept. Katta kept well away from Stefan. She sat by the window and looked out. There had been a procession to watch. The bells had stopped ringing, all save one, which tolled solemnly as the procession slowly wound its way around the harbour. She watched it come. At its front was a statue of an angel, all golden robes and feathers. The men who carried it on their shoulders shuffled under its weight. Its wings were stretched towards the sea. Boys in church robes swinging smoking censers had gone before it and priests in their robes had come behind. In the crowd that followed, people carried small statues and paintings of the angel, which they held up to be blessed.

But it wasn't the angel that had made Katta stare, though that was rich and gold, and they dipped it down to touch the water where the ice had been broken for it; it was the Duke of Felissehaven. Koenig pointed him out to her. He was wearing a robe finer than any other man's, with the Council of the City walking slowly behind him. People bowed as he passed, and it struck Katta, looking down from her window, that it wasn't respect or love that made them do it. It was fear. She could feel it pass like a wave through the crowd beneath her, and when she saw his face, she understood why. It was hard and

261

empty and merciless. As he walked, he looked at the people, turning his head slowly one way, then the other, and they quailed before him.

It hadn't always been so, Koenig told her. There'd been a time when the Duke had been loved. But that had changed ten or eleven years past. He'd been ill, they said. And now he was cruel like this, and no one dared oppose him. There was a length of rope and a dark drop for any that did.

It was his face that she remembered long after the people had gone. If it hadn't fixed her attention so much, she might have seen in the procession another face, one that she already knew – that of the Duke's physician – moon-shaped, and carrying a silver-topped cane.

Dark had already fallen when Koenig finally woke Mathias. He had let him sleep all day, but even then it wasn't enough. Mathias might have slept on for hours yet. Still on the edge of that deeply drugged sleep, uncomplaining, he allowed himself to be dressed and wrapped in his coat. Then, with a burning flare to light their way, Koenig led them through the cold streets. There was ice underfoot. Katta walked beside Mathias with her arm through his. She wasn't sure if he was really awake; he was walking as though in a dream. Stefan walked on the other side of her. She didn't like the feeling of that at all, but there was nothing she could do about it. Koenig didn't speak. She could see his face set hard in the light of the flare, and wondered what it was that he was thinking.

She recognized some of the streets – The Bear, the street where she'd had to run from the man. Then it was all new. They crossed the small bridge into the dark narrow court that led to the house where Jacob lived. The candles in the hall and on the stairs had been put out. They climbed through the darkness, Koenig holding the flickering flare. When they came to the landing, Koenig tapped on the old man's door and called his name, but there was no answer. He called again but there wasn't a sound from the room.

He glanced at Stefan, then pushed on the door; it opened.

The room was cold and dark. Jacob sat in his chair with his head tipped forward. He looked as though he were asleep. Koenig held the flare higher and said his name, but Jacob didn't move. So he put his hand under the old man's chin and lifted his face.

21

The Writing on the Wall

Katta had seen dead men before. She had even seen men who'd been hanged. She'd told herself that they were only asleep and had looked away. When she closed her eyes at night, she'd tried not to remember their faces, or the blood, but no matter how much she tried, she always did. She didn't want to look at Jacob now, but she couldn't help it. He sat in his dirty chair, in the flickering light, his head lolling back on his neck.

She couldn't say what it was, but there was something that dragged her eyes back to him and made her look.

Koenig closed the shutters. He told Stefan to stand by the door and keep watch. As he did so, Mathias slowly shook his head. The room about him had suddenly begun to make sense. It felt as though a blanket of sleep was being lifted away. Either Tashka's drug must have run its course, or he was becoming more used to it – because Koenig had given him enough to make him sleep for a week. He blinked and stared at Jacob, not realizing yet who it was.

'Who is that man?' he said slowly.

The sound of his voice made Katta turn round. She could see in the flickering light that his skin was grey and there was a sheen to it, but he was awake. If they had to run now, then he might be able to run too.

He wasn't looking at her though. He was looking at Jacob.

'Why is he pointing?' he said.

Katta turned to Jacob again; then she realized that was it – the thing that had made her look. She just hadn't understood what she was seeing until Mathias said it.

Jacob had one hand across his chest. But his other hand was on the arm of the chair and that was what was wrong. Strangled men would claw with both hands at a rope around their neck, dig their fingers into it until their heels drummed on the floor as the last scraps of breath were throttled out of them.

But not Jacob.

He could have pulled at the cord with only one thumbless hand because the other was gripping tightly onto the arm of the chair. Tightly, that is, save for one finger.

'He's pointing,' she said.

Koenig turned round and looked at her, then at Jacob.

'At the wall,' she said. 'Look. He's pointing.'

And he was.

Koenig bent over the dead man and followed the line that his finger made, but there was nothing to see.

'Maybe it's inside the wall,' said Katta.

He knelt down, moving the flare to and fro, the better to see. 'No,' he said. 'There's something scratched here. A name and a date – two dates. It's a woman's name and two dates.'

'Maybe it's when she lived here,' said Mathias. He'd screwed his eyes closed again, but he understood what was happening.

Koenig shook his head. 'No,' he said. 'They are big dates. This must be when she lived and when she died.'

He bent closer. The name – Gelein Merlevede –

was so lightly scratched in the plaster that unless you knew it was there, you wouldn't see it at all.

'There's more,' he said.

He narrowed his eyes and moved the flame nearer. For several moments he didn't say anything. Then he looked up at Katta. 'It says, *My loving wife Gelein Merlevede.*'

'What's that mean?' she said.

This time, Koenig smiled, but he didn't answer.

'How do we know it's to do with him?' said Mathias.

At the door, Stefan hissed them quiet. Something had moved on the landing, but it was only a cat.

Koenig lowered his voice. 'Because it's what he was pointing at when he died,' he said.

Straightening and standing up, Koenig began searching about. He picked up a dirty spoon from the table and scratched at the wall with its edge until there was nothing of the writing to be seen.

'Maybe he was trying to tell us,' he said. 'Or maybe he was just trying to save his own life – he told me that's what knowing about the other piece of paper was worth. But whoever killed him didn't see it, or the writing wouldn't be there. They'd have scratched it off.'

'What does it mean?' said Katta.

'It means that Gelein Merlevede has the other piece of paper.'

She looked at him blankly.

'It's an inscription on a gravestone,' said Koenig. 'Find her grave, and you find the other part of Meiserlann's paper.'

'Is that all there is to it?' asked Mathias.

'No,' said Koenig.

He moved Stefan aside and, opening the door, looked out into the dark of the landing, holding the flare up so that he could see the stairs above and below.

'You have to do what Jacob didn't do,' he said.

'What's that?' said Mathias.

Koenig turned and looked at him. 'Stay alive.'

They went through the dark, empty streets, back to the inn, Katta and Mathias jumping at every shadow. When Koenig shut the door of the room, he put a chair behind it, so that it couldn't be opened. Then he told them to sleep – it was already the dead hours of the night. He blew out the candles and settled himself into a corner. By the moonlight through the long window, Katta could just make out his shape, see the blue glint on the barrel of the pistol he held in his lap. She was so tired. She tried to think of good things happening to her – of finding riches and treasures, of the procession of the golden angel with bells ringing and people in the crowd, but all she could see when she shut her eyes was the face of the Duke, and of Jacob, dead in his dirty chair. As sleep opened its arms for her, it was their faces that followed her into its darkness and filled every part of her dreams.

'Wake up!' said Koenig.

He was shaking her. She blinked. The room was full of morning light. Mathias and Stefan were eating bread at the big table.

'You needed sleep,' he said. 'Now you must get up. There are things to do.'

'Like what?' she said.

He didn't answer her. He was impatient to be out of the room, she could see that. He picked up the saddlebags and strapped them shut. Then he took the bread that hadn't already been eaten and pushed it into his coat pocket.

'Come. Now,' he said.

Stefan picked up his bag.

'Where are we going?' said Katta.

'You ask too many questions,' said Koenig.

'It's what you do when people don't tell you nothin',' she said.

But he didn't pay her any attention. He checked the pistols and, putting one of them inside his coat, slipped the other beneath the strap of a saddlebag.

'You already know,' he said when he'd finished.

Then she remembered Gelein Merlevede and the writing on the wall. 'We're going to find a grave?' she said, and shuddered.

'No,' said Koenig, and only then did he look at her. 'We're going to find a doctor.'

He led them down to the stables where Razor was tethered, and put the saddlebags on the ground beneath the horse's head, then covered them over with straw. The stableboy pretended not to watch, but he did it too casually, and Koenig saw.

'Don't even think of touching them,' he said. He ran his hand along the glossy side of the big horse. 'He kicked the last man who was stupid enough to do that.' He put his face close to that of the boy. 'They never found one half of his head.'

The boy grinned. Then, uncertain of the joke, he

looked from Koenig to the huge horse. It turned its head and he could see the wild white of its eye and then realized that, just maybe, Koenig hadn't been joking.

Koenig patted him on the cheek. 'Just leave them where they are,' he said menacingly, and gave the boy a coin. 'Another one,' he added, 'if you are still alive when I come back.'

Katta hadn't believed Koenig the day before when he'd said he'd take Mathias to a doctor. She'd thought he'd only said it to keep her quiet until he had the chance to meet Jacob again. But she was wrong.

The doctor was a nervous young man, fresh from the University Medical School. His treatment room was the best he could manage on an empty pocket. Mathias sat grey-faced and shirtless on the examining table, his legs dangling over the edge. He made small keening sounds as the doctor ran his hands over the places that hurt.

'This boy should be in a hospital,' the doctor said.

'We don't have that choice,' answered Koenig. 'What can you do for him?'

'His ribs are broken. He is not well.'

'I think we already know that,' said Koenig coldly.

'I asked, *What can you do for him?*'

Koenig had an unsettling effect on people. It was those hard, unwavering grey eyes. The doctor might have been a rabbit in front of a wolf.

'I can stitch him,' he began hesitantly. 'Pull the broken ribs straight – they are against his lung; that is why he is so grey. I can strap him.'

'Will that make him any better?' said Koenig.

'Yes,' said the doctor uncertainly. Then, more confidently, 'Yes, it will. But he needs to rest.'

Koenig shook his head.

The doctor didn't seem to know what to say next, whether to argue the point or not, but Koenig stood, hard-faced, and said nothing. In the end the doctor let out a long breath.

'I'll do what I can,' he said.

'Good,' said Koenig and smiled. He managed to look even more dangerous when he did.

Mathias watched uncomfortably as the doctor opened a cupboard and, laying out a tray, began to make his things ready.

'If you die in this city,' said Koenig, 'who knows where you are buried?'

The doctor put the tray down. 'Your family would, I suppose,' he said hesitantly.

Koenig frowned impatiently.

'Oh, I see what you mean,' said the doctor quickly. 'You mean records. Well, that depends where you are buried – which quarter of the city. They each have their own records.'

'How many cemeteries are there?' said Koenig.

'Four? Five? Not counting the crypts – you know, beneath the churches. And the ossuaries – but that would only be bones.'

'How many crypts?'

The young man blew out his cheeks. 'Dozens,' he said, shaking his head.

Katta caught Koenig's eye. 'Where would you be buried,' she said, 'if you was to die near The Bear?'

'I don't think I know where that is,' said the doctor.

He wasn't used to being questioned by scruffy girls, but Koenig saw at once what she meant.

'Near the harbour,' he said. 'There's a river and a bridge.'

'Oh,' said the doctor. He picked up his tray again and checked that he had the right instruments on it. 'That – would – be,' he said slowly, 'Saints Maximilian and Mary. Or one of the crypts,' he added. 'Yes. Maximilian and Mary.'

He put his hand on Mathias's good shoulder and smiled at him, then looked up at Koenig. 'Now,' he said. 'You need to hold the boy.'

'You are very clever,' said Koenig when they were in the street again.

'Stands to reason,' said Katta. 'If it was Jacob what hid it, he wouldn't have gone far, would he, see? So it has to be the nearest one.'

She felt very pleased with herself. She might not know what was going to happen next, but she was a part of it now, and Koenig might need her yet.

But she wouldn't have felt so pleased if at that moment she'd turned round and seen the look on Stefan's face. He was thinking that he could have been clever like her too. That he could have thought where Jacob had hidden the paper, if he'd been given the chance. But he hadn't, and it was Katta who had taken it from him.

Always Katta.

Well, he could see to that.

Mathias looked more grey than he had done before, but the doctor said that was to be expected. His shoulder had been cleaned and stitched. The broken ribs pulled, painfully, back into their right place with a piece of wire. Now he had to heal: all that he needed was rest. It was hardly what he was going to get, though.

They walked across the city, through the winding alleys, until they found the cemetery of the Saints Maximilian and Mary. There was a high stone wall about it and it was closed with heavy iron gates. Koenig pushed the gates open. There was snow and ice on the paths. It was a soulless place. There was not a sound. People would not come here other than to bury their dead, or be buried. There were no noises of the living city – of people or barking dogs. It was as if the sounds had died too. There were only the dead here, and they did not speak.

They stood together in the cold, looking at the rows of snow-covered graves and tombs. Some had iron railings around them; others were broken and fallen down. There was a chill wind. Katta shivered. She didn't like graves – didn't want to die and lie with the worms beneath all that suffocating earth.

'There's hundreds,' she said.

'We go different ways,' said Koenig. 'We each take a row. And we look.'

'I'll go with him,' said Katta quickly. She put her

arm through Mathias's. 'He might need help.'

'All right,' said Koenig. 'Call out if you find it.'

Holding onto him, Katta led Mathias between the graves. She broke sticks of ivy from a headstone and used them to brush the snow away from the letters.

'You'll have to read it,' she said.

Mathias carefully traced the words with his finger-tips, his lips moving slowly as he did so, but it wasn't the one. Nor was the next. Nor the next. Nor the next.

Mathias felt as though they'd been looking for hours. He was cold and sick. He looked around at all the graves. It was hopeless. He could see Koenig far away amongst the tombs close by the wall. Stefan was sitting on a headstone, tapping a stick on his boots.

'It could be anywhere,' said Mathias, and there was despair in his voice. 'It might not even be here.'

But Katta was sure it was. The only thing she could think of now was finding it.

'All we gotta do is look,' she said. 'Whatever it is, he'd have hid it in the nearest place, and that's here.' She took his arm again and drew him along the path to where the next row of graves began. 'Come on,' she said.

And she was right.

Gelein Merlevede had been buried without fuss. A simple stone. It had fallen sideways and was half grown over. It could have been any grave. And that perhaps was the point. It didn't stand out as special. You would have to look for it to find it. Katta brushed the snow from it, as she had done a hundred times already. Her fingers were cold and raw. She was already walking on to the next stone when she realized that Mathias hadn't followed her. She looked back at him and saw at once from the way that he was standing, staring at the stone, that they'd found the one they were looking for. She ran back towards him. He glanced up at her, then back at the stone. Her heart was pounding. Running his finger along the line of frost-worn letters, he said each word slowly so as to be quite sure he hadn't made a mistake.

'*My loving wife Gelein Merlevede.* It's her,' he said. 'This is the one.'

Then he looked at Katta and she knew what he meant without him saying a word. Whatever the secret was, they'd found it – and they didn't have to tell.

Koenig was still searching. They could see him, moving among the stones far away to their left. If he looked up now, he'd know straight away that they'd found it.

Mathias couldn't see where Stefan was. He turned one way then the other, but Stefan had been bending down reading a stone only a dozen rows away. As he stood up, he happened to look straight at Mathias and the expression on his face told him everything. He started shouting, 'Koenig! Koenig!' and began to run towards Mathias, pointing and beckoning to Koenig as he ran.

When Koenig reached the place where they stood, he moved Mathias to one side and roughly brushed the last of the frost from the inscription with his hand. His breath left cold clouds in the air.

'*Gelein Merlevede,*' he said.

He ran his hand around the edges of the stone, feeling for any crack or crevice where something might be hidden. But there was nothing there. Standing up, he kicked the snow away, clearing the grave, but there was just bare, frozen earth and yellowed grass.

'It must be in it,' he said.

He cast his eyes around. Beside the cemetery gates was a small stone hut.

Newly dead bodies were valuable things. The medical schools paid well for them. They didn't always ask too carefully where they had come from. That's why the hut was there. It stopped people from digging up the fresh body. Family or friends could shelter there and watch over the grave. After a few days a body was no use to anyone any more. Then they could go home, knowing that it wouldn't end up on a medical school's slab. The gravedigger used it as well, for his tools, and that was what Koenig was looking for. He began walking towards the hut.

'What are you going to do?' said Katta.

There was a tremor in her voice. Stefan heard it

and grinned. About them, the shadows were deepening, the sky beginning to redden as the day closed.

'We wait until it's dark,' said Koenig.

'Then what?'

Stefan pushed his face close to hers. '*Leje tel lankos*,' he whispered.

She looked at Koenig but she already knew what the words meant.

'We dig it up.'

22
The Small Lead Box

The stone floor of the hut was raised higher than the cemetery it looked out upon. This made it easier for people to watch over the graves. There were three steps up. A shutter served as a window. Inside, against one wall, the gravedigger had propped his pick and long-handled spade. His ropes and boards were there too. There was a bench, a stool, and the stub of a candle in a niche, but nothing else. It was colder inside than out.

Katta and Mathias sat on the bench, pressed against each other for warmth. They watched the sky through the shuttered window as it steadily deepened in colour. Stefan sat at the bottom of the steps. As it grew darker, he came back in. He lifted the pick from the wall and began chipping holes in the stone floor with it. It made a hollow, empty thump.

Thump.

'Tell him to stop doing that,' said Katta.

Stefan looked up at her and said something to Koenig in Burner. Koenig glanced at Katta, then away.

'What did he say?' she said.

'It does not matter,' said Koenig.

Stefan grinned at her. It made her want to slap his face.

'I want to know,' she said.

Koenig didn't answer. He went down the steps and stood looking out into the frosty air as the last of the light dwindled and faded. Mathias put his hand on Katta's sleeve – she knew what he meant. She took a deep breath and turned her back on Stefan.

Thump, went the pick again.

She tried to shut her ears to it, but she couldn't. It only made what she was thinking worse. It was wrong to open a grave, she knew that. If you did, you let dead things come out – rotting and eyeless – and they would creep after you for ever; even if you hid in a church, they'd scratch at the door outside. She'd been told once by someone who knew. She could feel her palms damp, her mouth like ash. She wiped her hands on her coat. What if the paper were

283

right in the coffin? What if Gelein Merlevede were holding it in her hand? She looked at Koenig, standing in the fading light. It wouldn't stop him, she thought; he'd dig it up all the same. But maybe, if she didn't stand too close, it wouldn't come after her.

Koenig came back up the steps. 'The moon is rising,' he said, taking the spade from the wall.

They walked through the dark cemetery. Koenig went in front, Katta and Mathias followed. Stefan came behind. Katta didn't like the feeling of him being there, behind her. She tried walking more slowly so that he might go past, but Stefan slowed too. He made sure that he was always behind her.

The moon cast dark shadows amongst the tombs. There was no sound. Only the dead could make quiet like that. Katta pulled the collar of her coat high up around her chin and closed her eyes as she walked between the graves. Then Koenig stopped. They had come to the stone. She tried not to think of the long-dead woman wrapped in her shroud only feet below them. She tried not to think of what was going to happen next.

Koenig kicked the frost from the grass, spat on his hands and lifted the heavy pick. He said something to Stefan, then in one long curve he swung the pick into the ice-hard ground. It made barely a mark. He lifted it and swung again; this time it bit in, and he worked the point backwards and forwards until an icy scab of earth lifted away. Then he swung again. The sound of the pick carried on the cold air. He stopped to listen, but if anyone had heard, no one came.

Koenig and Stefan took the digging turn and turn about. The ground was frozen so hard that they might as well have tried to chip away at stone. But, scab by scab, the ground gave under the pick, and what was first a shallow scrape became deeper, then

wider and deeper. They began to lift earth away with the shovel. Katta wondered what it must be like for Gelein Merlevede in the cold dark of her soundless coffin, hearing the scrape of the shovel and the scuff of the pick digging down towards her. She tried not to think, but the picture in her head would not go away. The dead woman was waiting for them down in the dark, cold ground. Koenig climbed out of the hole, and Stefan got in, lifted the pick and started again.

Mathias began to shake. 'I'm so cold,' he said.

Katta put her arms around him. It gave her something to do and took her eyes away from the digging.

Stefan was almost up to his waist in the hole when, with a thump, the pick hit something wooden and hollow.

It was the coffin.

The lid had long since rotted. As Stefan shovelled the earth clear, the wood suddenly gave way under his weight. His foot went straight through and into the coffin beneath. He must have thought that something had grabbed him. He gave a yell and scrambled, whimpering, out of the grave, trying to brush away the shreds of shroud that clung to his leg. Koenig caught hold of him and shook him hard.

'*Shtahl!*' he hissed.

The cold air was thick with a stale stink from the broken coffin. Crumbs of soil were rolling like peppercorns down into the gaping black hole that Stefan's foot had made in the lid.

Koenig let go of him and jumped down into the grave. Standing astride the lid, he began to lever at it with the pick. Katta couldn't bear it any more. She could feel the last shreds of her nerve going. Mathias had already turned away. He couldn't look. Koenig was pulling slivers of wood away.

'Don't!' she cried.

He looked up at her.

'It won't be in the coffin! How could he have put it in the coffin? She's been dead for years!'

All she had been trying to do was stop him pulling the shroud away from that awful face, but even as she said the words, she realized that she was right.

'How could he have dug up a whole grave?' she said.

Koenig realized it too. He looked down into the hole, then up again at her. 'It has to be in the ground,' he said. 'Not in the coffin.'

He climbed out of the grave and, taking the shovel from where Stefan had thrown it, began to sift through the pile of earth they had already emptied from the hole, but there was nothing there. He got down into the hole again and, with the edge of the shovel, began to scrape the sides of it clean, running his fingers through each fresh shower of earth that fell away. He had been doing it for only a moment when he dropped the shovel and stood brushing earth away from something that he was holding in his hand. It was a small box, not much bigger than his palm, but it was heavy, made of lead. He climbed out of the grave.

'We need light,' he said, and began to walk back towards the hut.

Katta looked at the dark, gaping hole. 'You can't leave it like this,' she said.

But Koenig didn't answer. He carried on walking.

'Koenig!'

Stefan pushed his face close to hers and swore at her – she didn't need to know the words to understand what they meant. He put his arm though Mathias's and, pulling him along, followed after Koenig.

They couldn't leave it like this. Something would climb out. Katta picked up the shovel; it was heavy and the handle was ice-cold. She started to tip earth back in. It rattled down onto the coffin lid. In the dark, all around, she could feel the silence waiting.

'I'm sorry,' she said.

She kept saying the words quickly, over and over again, as she tipped more earth in.

'I'm sorry, I'm so sorry, I'm so sorry.'

Then something moved in the bottom of the grave. It was only the broken lid falling into the coffin under the weight of the earth, but it was enough. The last of Katta's nerve gave way and she screamed. Dropping the shovel, she fled, running blindly through the dark, not sure which way the others had gone, tripping and falling as she went.

Stefan had lit the candle stub. She saw the flickering light and ran towards it, falling up the steps into the hut, then standing breathless in the doorway, staring back out into the dark, but there was nothing moving, nothing coming after her. Maybe she had done enough. She could feel her racing heart skipping beats. When she turned round, Koenig was crouching in the candlelight, prising the box open with the tip of his knife. He glanced up at her, and even as he did so, the box opened like two halves of an oyster shell and something dropped through his fingers onto the floor.

Mathias picked it up and held it to the light of the candle.

It was a small square of folded paper.

Koenig swept the top of the bench clear with the side of his hand, then took the paper from Mathias, unfolded it and flattened it out. It was just like the other piece, torn in just the same way – and just like the other piece it was completely blank.

For a moment no one spoke. Koenig picked up the two halves of the box and shook them, but there was nothing else inside.

'This can't be it,' said Mathias.

'This must be it,' said Koenig.

He reached into his coat and, taking out the leather wallet, pulled the other piece of paper from it and laid the two pieces side by side. The torn edges matched exactly, but they were both blank.

He looked up at Mathias.

Mathias stared at the pieces of paper and frowned. It had to be a trick. He knew it. But you have to make tricks work – he knew that too. He tried to imagine what Gustav would have done – there on the stage with all their eyes upon him.

Hesitantly he leaned forward and clapped his hands.

And then it happened.

It was like paper dropped flat into a fire – it takes a moment to catch, then burns from the middle out. A small blue-green flame ran along the line where the pieces touched. It crept slowly outwards over them both, but it had no heat. Where it passed it left a pattern of lines behind. They watched, open-mouthed, as the flame moved.

'It's making writing,' said Mathias.

'No,' said Koenig. 'Look.'

The flame reached the furthest edges of the paper, and as it touched the wood of the bench, it flickered and went out. Koenig lifted the candle nearer.

It wasn't writing that had been left behind.

Drawn across the two pieces of paper was the outline of a building – like a plan of its floor – but that wasn't all.

In one corner, marking an exact place, was a small black cross.

23

Across the Ice

While the flame had burned it filled the hut with a smell of honey and resin. It lingered in the air. It was the same smell that clung to Gustav's clothes after he had done those unfathomable tricks – the ones that only Mathias ever saw. Mathias had asked Gustav about it only once, and Gustav had gripped Mathias's face with fingers like a vice, squeezing it so hard that it hurt.

'Mustn't be too clever, must we?' he'd said.

And Mathias knew better than to ask again, so what that smell was he never knew.

But now it took him back to Lutsmann's travelling show, to the curtains thrown wide and the crowds in the flickering torchlight. He looked through the doorway at the moonlit graves, half expecting to see Gustav, with his white face, standing beside one of them. But there was only darkness and silence.

Then he realized that Koenig was asking him a question.

'How did it do that?'

He could only shake his head. 'I don't know,' he said.

'Do you know what this is?'

Mathias looked at the lines on the paper and shook his head again. Stefan leaned forward, his dark eyes glittering in the candlelight.

'*Kruzka?*' he said.

'It might be,' said Koenig.

'What did he say?' asked Katta.

'A church,' said Koenig, looking up at her. 'Maybe it's a church.' He drew his finger along the lines. 'This could be the nave or the altar.'

'Or a garden,' said Katta. 'That might be walls round a garden and a path.'

Her eyes were wide with excitement. It was as though, filled with the promise of riches, she'd forgotten everything else. She looked at each of them in turn.

'It's treasure, innit?' she whispered.

But that still made no sense to Mathias. He was looking not at her, but at Koenig. He wanted to know what Koenig was thinking.

Koenig had wet his fingers to snuff out the candle stub and Mathias caught his eye. It was only a glance, but it was enough. Whatever it might be that the paper showed, Koenig didn't think it was treasure either.

They spent the night in the hut. Koenig woke them before first light – not that they'd slept much. He wanted them to be away before anyone chanced upon the open grave of Gelein Merlevede.

What Koenig planned to do was find a high place from which they could look down on the city. There were squares and alleyways with good views over the streets and roofs below – they'd passed places like that the day before. Maybe they could see from there a garden or courtyard that matched what Gustav had drawn on the paper. There was nothing to say that it was even in the city, but the chances had to be that it was.

'What if it's a room inside a house?' asked Mathias.

'Then we won't see it,' said Koenig.

'*Kruzka*,' said Stefan.

'It's not goin' to be hidden in a church,' said Katta.

She didn't want Stefan to be the one who was right. But Koenig didn't dismiss it.

'It depends what it is,' he said.

There were churches enough for them to look in as they worked their way up through the town. Each one was cold, and heavy with the thick smell of incense. From the darkness of the roofs gilded angels looked down, and above every altar hung the blue and silver banner of the Duke of Felissehaven, reminder – as if any were needed – of where earthly power really lay.

In each church they looked in, they tried to match what they could see with what Gustav had drawn, but nothing ever came close. There was always some part that was different, something that wasn't the same. And it was drawn so carefully, so exactly, that they had no doubt they would know the place the moment they found it.

They had no better luck when they tried looking from the highest places down onto the roofs and courtyards below. They stood in the cold wind, pointing and comparing, but the day wore on and they found nothing.

The bell for the last service of the afternoon had been rung as they walked through the doors of a church near the top of the town. The priest had already begun the prayers. A single candle burned in a red glass lantern above the altar, but there was only a handful of people in the church. Koenig dipped his fingers into the bowl of water by the door and crossed himself. When Stefan did the same, Katta copied them and nodded to Mathias that he should do it too. Then they sat together in a pew and waited until the service was done. Katta didn't know what she was supposed to do. She sat peeping through her fingers at the bent heads of the people as they prayed.

When it was over, Koenig waited until the church had emptied and the priest was trimming the altar candles.

'Father,' he called. 'A question, if I may?'

Pulling the pieces of paper from the leather wallet, he held them out for the priest to see, but carefully so that his thumb was over the mark that Gustav had made.

'It was my father's drawing,' he said. 'I always thought it had to be the church where he was married, but I've never known if it was true and he's long gone now. Could it be a church in the city?'

Katta stared at Koenig – it was bad to lie in a

church – but he didn't look at her.

The priest looked carefully at the pieces of paper that Koenig held. For a moment he said nothing. Then he shook his head.

'It is not a church that I know.'

'You are sure?'

He smiled at Koenig and shook his head again. 'I know them all. I'm sorry.'

'Knew it wasn't,' said Katta under her breath as they walked towards the door. She took a sideways look at Stefan. '*Kruzka*,' she said.

They'd almost reached the door when the priest called after them. 'Are you sure it was where he was married?' he said.

Koenig stopped and turned. 'Why?'

'Because the only thing it could be, I suppose, is the monastery chapel.'

'On the island?' said Koenig.

The priest held his hand out, beckoning to Koenig to bring him the paper so that he could see it again.

'It's not all ruins,' he said. 'Some of it has been carried away, but the chapel is still there, and one or two of the other buildings. It's just the roofs and floors that have fallen in.'

He looked at the paper again. 'Yes,' he said. 'I can see it now.' He drew his finger along the lines, showing them each detail as he spoke. 'These are the alcoves, and that is the window, and that is the door.'

He looked up at Koenig. 'That is the Chapel of Saint Becca the Old,' he said. 'It would not have been a place for a wedding.'

'On the island?' said Koenig again.

'Yes,' said the priest. 'On the island.'

Stefan turned to Katta and grinned at her. '*Kruzka*,' he said.

He'd been right.

There was only one way to reach the place, and that was to walk out across the ice. No boat could get there until the thaw came with the spring. But they had to wait until dark. Too many eyes would see. Too many questions would be asked.

So they waited.

They didn't go back to the inn. They sat instead with their backs to the harbour wall, staring out across the ice, watching as the last traces of colour drained from the sky and, one by one, lanterns were lit on the barges in the harbour, and on the ships at anchor out in the sound. Koenig had been back to fetch one of the bags from the stable – Stefan's; it was all they needed. Now he sat with it between his feet, looking across the frozen bay as the light failed. He could just make out the distant shape of the island against the darker line of the sea. The priest had said that from the shore there were steps cut into the rocks – the chapel stood on its own above the cliff.

Whatever Gustav's secret was, that was where they would find it.

Katta sat close to Mathias. She'd been full of the promise of treasure, but now, sitting in the gathering dark looking out across the ice, she was not so sure.

What if it had been Leiter who'd hidden it? What if that's what it had been about all the time – not finding what Mathias had taken, but making sure that no one else ever did? Was that why they'd killed Jacob? Was that what Mathias had been trying to tell her?

A cold thought went like ice down her spine. She pulled at Mathias's sleeve. 'What if he knows we've found it?'

But it was Koenig who answered. 'He doesn't,' he said. 'But he can't be sure, can he?'

'So what will he do?' said Katta.

Koenig stood up and picked up the bag. 'What would you do?' he said.

Mathias had been sitting staring out at the island, turning that same question over in his mind. He already knew the answer. 'I'd go and look,' he said quietly.

'Then we'd better make sure we get there first,' said Koenig.

It took them two hours. As they walked across the hard-packed ice, the lights of Felissehaven steadily dwindled to a shimmer behind them. When they came to the shore, Koenig lit a small lantern. It had a shutter that half hid the light it threw. At first they couldn't find the steps. It was only after working their way back and forth amongst the rocks that they saw them, winding up into the blackness. Koenig closed the lantern and, with only the moon to light their way, they began to climb up the rough wet cleft of stone.

It was a hard climb, almost too much for Mathias. But at the top they stepped out onto level ground, and there was the monastery laid out in silhouette ruins before them, its broken walls open to the sky.

At the cliff edge, some distance from the others, one solitary building stood facing out across the sea.

'*Voy,*' said Stefan, pulling at Mathias's sleeve. '*Kruzka.*'

They went in silence through the empty cloisters, picking their way between the fallen blocks of stone that lay on the ground. In the distance they could hear the muffled thump of the sea breaking over the margins of the ice.

Had they turned round then and looked back towards Felissehaven, they might have seen the light coming steadily out across the ice towards them.

The door to the chapel was closed. Stefan took the

heavy iron ring in both hands and twisted it, but nothing happened. He leaned all his weight against the wood. At first it didn't move, then Koenig put his shoulder to it as well and, with a crack, the hinges began to grind slowly open.

Inside, everything was quiet. Part of the chapel roof had fallen in. A single shaft of moonlight dropped between the roof beams and onto the stone floor. Koenig unshuttered the lantern and held it up. As he did so, angels seemed to leap out of the darkness around them, but they were only paintings on the plaster of the walls – their faces and wings salt-stained and decayed.

Koenig slipped the pack from his shoulders and, dropping it to the floor, pulled the pieces of paper from inside his coat. Holding the lantern, he began to walk slowly along the walls, past each dark alcove that was drawn on the paper. 'This is the place,' he said.

Until then, they hadn't been sure. The priest might have been wrong. It might have been another building, or another city. But it wasn't. This was what Gustav had drawn.

Koenig held the lantern higher and its light fell upon the farthest end of the chapel. 'It's over there,' he said.

There was nothing to see. But when they held the lantern close to the floor, they could make out stones where the edges were marked and scuffed by tools, as though they had been lifted and laid again.

Stefan slipped out of the lamplight into the darkness. When he came back, he was carrying the pack. Koenig undid the straps and, pulling a metal bar from it, settled himself over the stones and began to lever them up, one by one. Stefan dragged each one away as it came free. They had moved only a few when they uncovered a step, and then another one below it, but the rest was filled with rocks.

'It must lead to the crypt,' said Koenig.

It took time to clear away the rocks. Katta pulled her coat about her and sat with Mathias at the edge of the pool of light – he had hardly any strength left. It was like watching the grave of Gelein Merlevede being opened again. She tried not to think of the dead woman in the dark, or what it was that had been hidden here, but it was no use.

'Make them stop,' she said.

But Mathias just shook his head. It was too late for that now.

The patch of moonlight that fell through the roof crept slowly across the floor. Stefan had taken off his thick coat and, breathing heavily, was holding the lantern for Koenig. A huge pile of stones lay on the ground behind him. He looked up at Mathias.

'*Voy*,' he said.

Stiffly Mathias stood up and walked to the edge of the hole. Koenig was standing at the bottom of a shallow flight of steps. There was a low doorway in front of him. It was barred with a thick metal grille. He was prising the ends of it from the stone.

Katta came and stood by Mathias. As she did so, the last bar of metal came free and the grille swung heavily sideways and dropped with a clang onto the steps. Stefan handed the lantern down to Koenig, who put his hand to the door and pushed.

As it opened, stale cold air breathed out of the darkness and the lantern flame guttered.

'Come on,' said Mathias quietly and, taking hold of Katta's hand, he led her down the steps.

In the shadows of the lantern light, beneath a low vaulted ceiling, lay the empty stone coffins that had once held the abbots of the monastery of St Becca the Old. Their bones, along with the relics of that saint, had long since been taken to the churches of Felissehaven. Each stone lid lay cracked and broken on the floor next to its coffin. Then the flame guttered again, and Mathias began to back towards the door.

Gustav's secret was in here, and it wasn't treasure.

'Them two have still got lids,' said Katta. Her voice was no more than a whisper.

Koenig held up the lantern. In the furthest shadows of the crypt, two of the coffins had been closed again. He put down the light and fitted the end of the metal bar into the crack beneath the lid of the nearest one. It was too heavy for him to move.

'Stefan. *Vasi.*'

Stefan pushed past Katta, and she watched as he and Koenig leaned all their weight on the metal. There was a slow grating sound and the lid moved. The small room filled with a foul stink.

'Again!' said Koenig.

Inch by inch, they worked with the bar, levering the lid aside. When it had moved enough, Koenig picked up the lantern and held it over the open coffin.

The man had been dead for a long time, but his face, taut and transparent, had hardly decayed at all. The cold, airless crypt had seen to that. There was a deep, bloodless gash from one side of his neck to the other where his throat had been cut.

305

Katta stared.

She had seen that face before. Hard and empty and merciless. It had stayed in her mind long after the procession had gone.

It was the face of the Duke of Felissehaven.

'The other one,' said Koenig.

Stefan jammed the metal bar into the other coffin and they began to lever at the lid. This time the stone cracked, and they tipped the broken part onto the ground.

Another man lay there, and Katta recognized him too. It was the tall churchman she had seen walk from the opera house with Dr Leiter on the night of the Festival of the Angel, mask dangling from his fingers by its ribbons.

'But they're alive,' she said. 'I se—'

Koenig didn't let her finish what she had begun to say. He closed his hand so hard across her mouth that she couldn't breathe. She began to struggle, but then she heard it too.

The click of stone on stone.

Someone was in the chapel above them.

Koenig took his hand slowly away from Katta's mouth and closed the lantern shutter. He drew the pistol from his coat – in the darkness Katta heard the click as he cocked the hammer. Then he slipped past her, into the spill of blue moonlight that fell onto the bottom of the steps, and stopped and listened.

Nothing moved in the empty chapel. There was not a sound. Stefan's pack lay untouched next to the heap of stones. But Koenig knew what he had heard. Quiet as a cat, he went up the steps.

Katta and Mathias came slowly up the steps behind him. Stefan followed, still clutching the iron bar. Koenig motioned to them to wait. He was searching the darkness. As they watched, he began to walk across the floor, sweeping the pistol through every shadowed place. He had got halfway to the chapel door when some sixth sense made him look up, and in that instant Valter dropped from the rafters, hitting Koenig like a ton rock.

The back of Koenig's head cracked against the stone floor as he fell and the world exploded in blinding light. Valter was on him instantly, pinning him to the ground, beating the hand that held the pistol against the floor until Koenig's fingers cracked open and the pistol skittered away across the stones into the darkness. Koenig was trying to drive the heel of his hand under the dwarf's chin, but effortlessly Valter pulled it aside and smashed his head down into Koenig's face.

It had happened so quickly.

Stefan stood at the top of the stairs, eyes wide, stupidly clutching the iron bar.

'Help him!' shouted Katta.

But Stefan couldn't move. It was as though he was suddenly rooted to the spot. He was shaking, staring at Koenig and the dwarf. Katta tried to pull the bar from his hands, but he only looked at her wild-eyed; the more she pulled, the more he gripped hold of it.

She screamed at him, 'Give it to me!'

Koenig was on his feet, his face thick with blood. Valter had drawn a long curved knife from his coat and the two of them were slowly circling in the moonlight.

'Stefan! *Lavti!*' shouted Koenig.

But still Stefan couldn't move. It was Katta who wrenched the bar out of his hands and threw it across the floor towards Koenig. It rang like a bell as it landed on the stones midway between Koenig and Valter. As Koenig bent to pick it up, Valter slashed at his face, but in one movement Koenig dropped beneath the blade, his hand closed around the bar and he brought it slamming upwards into Valter's body. The dwarf staggered backwards.

'Run!' shouted Koenig.

Katta grabbed Mathias's hand and they fled towards the door. She could hear Stefan behind her. As she reached the doorway, Stefan pushed past, pulling Mathias after him, but she stopped and looked back.

'Run!' shouted Koenig again, and swung the bar at the dwarf.

She didn't need telling again. She lifted up her skirts and ran. Stefan and Mathias were already amongst the tumbled stones in the cloisters, Mathias bent double, Stefan pulling him along, but even as she ran after them, a noise like an angry wasp started in her head.

'No!' she whimpered. 'No!'

Running and whimpering, she reached the archway and stumbled into the moonlit cloister beyond it. All around her the world was breaking into flickering pinpricks of light.

'No!' She pulled herself to her feet and ran again.

The end of the passage had been blocked by a fallen wall. Stefan had climbed up into the narrow gap at the top. He was dragging Mathias after him, pushing him down into the darkness on the other side. He saw her and reached his hand down to pull her up.

But then he stopped.

In that moment she saw his face. She could see the long, ugly wound where she'd drawn the knife across it, and she knew what he was going to do. Pins of light were shimmering like a halo round his head.

'Please?' she said, and reached her hand up towards him.

But he'd already gone. She stood staring dumbly at the place where he'd been, and at the flickering lights that were closing in and filling it.

It had happened again.

She didn't know where she was. She could feel hard, cold ground against her cheek. Her skirt was soiled and wet against her legs. Then she saw a light, floating like a moth towards her. She tried to lift her head, but it was so heavy. She lay and watched as the moth light came nearer.

It was a lantern. Someone was holding a lantern.

He was almost on her. As he bent over her, a face slowly appeared out of the darkness and she closed her eyes, because she had no strength to do anything else.

Holding the lantern was Dr Leiter.

24

Death in the Chapel

Valter and Koenig circled in the moonlit chapel, their eyes following each other's every move. Valter held the long, razor-edged knife in his hand. Neither made a sound; each silently watched the other.

Then Valter suddenly turned, and the knife came slicing through the air towards Koenig's face. It was so fast. In that frozen instant Koenig saw the blade edgeways on and, behind it, Valter's filthy hair flung across his face. But Koenig was already swinging the iron bar upwards: it caught Valter on the side of the head and the dwarf went down, the knife skittering from his hand. Koenig was on him at once and, with the iron bar in both hands, he put it around Valter's throat, his knee in Valter's back, and began to choke the life out of him.

But Valter was strong. He put his hands to the iron bar and with sheer strength prised it inch by inch away from his throat. There was nothing Koenig could do to stop him. Like a circus wrestler, Valter suddenly jerked himself downwards and forward. The speed of it caught Koenig completely off balance and, the iron bar still in his hands, he went over Valter's shoulders and crashed into the hard stone floor.

Valter picked up the knife. Koenig was only just on his feet when Valter came on again, feinting and ducking beneath the swinging bar, driving Koenig backwards across the chapel with sweeping slashes that opened the thick Burner coat like paper.

For a moment they stood apart. The front of Koenig's coat was sodden with his blood. He was breathing hard, but he wasn't hurt as much as he pretended to be. He let the bar seem heavy in his hands, but all the while he was tensing his body, choosing his moment.

A slow grin spread across Valter's face, and that was when Koenig moved. The bar was only a blur through the air, but the dwarf saw it coming. He ducked beneath it and drove the knife hard into Koenig. Koenig reeled away. This time there was no pretence. Instinctively he put his arm across the wound. He tried to swing at Valter again, but the dwarf sucked himself back away from the bar and the knife passed across Koenig's chest and back with incredible speed.

Then Valter stood back, crouching, faintly weaving, watching Koenig's eyes. This was the part of the game he enjoyed the most. Watching the person die. He had played it a hundred times before. He knew what death looked like when it came, and he could see it now.

Koenig put his hand to the wound. It came away sticky with thick dark blood. He wiped it on the side of his coat and began to back slowly away from Valter, but his legs folded crookedly beneath him and he crumpled to the floor. He still held the bar in his hand, but now it felt like lead.

Valter slowly straightened and stood up. He stepped quietly forward and pulled the bar out of Koenig's unresisting hand as though he were a child and the bar a toy. He threw it away into the darkness. It rang as it hit the wall. There was a sudden brilliant light in Koenig's head as Valter bent down and hit him with the back of his hand, sending him sprawling across the chapel floor.

Koenig landed in a heap against a pile of fallen stones. He could feel their chill cold against his cheek. A voice in his head was telling him that he had to get up or die, but it was so far away. He opened his eyes. Valter was walking slowly towards him through the moonlight, the long, razor-edged knife in his hand. Koenig pushed himself to his knees. Tiny dots of light swam across the stone floor in front of him. But there was something else amongst them. He had been half lying across it. He looked at the shape stupidly, not knowing what it was. Then he understood.

Valter walked behind him. He leaned down and wound his short, stubby fingers in Koenig's hair, forcing his head back ready to cut his throat. As he did so, Koenig brought the pistol up from the floor, jammed it under Valter's chin and pulled the trigger.

The pistol ball blew the top of the dwarf's head clean off. The knife clattered to the floor. In the ringing silence that followed there was a sound that Koenig didn't understand, like falling confetti of a thousand tiny metal bells. Valter swayed, dropped to his knees and toppled forwards onto Koenig.

Koenig pushed the dead weight away. He put his

315

hand on a block of stone and struggled to his feet. His coat sagged with the weight of his blood. With his hand pressed to his side, he walked unsteadily towards the open chapel door, leaned against its broken frame and breathed in the freezing night air.

Mathias had run blindly through the ruins. He had no idea where Katta or Stefan had gone. He just ran. When he couldn't run any more, he found a small dark crevice and crawled into it. He lay squeezed against the stones, listening, but all he could hear was the sound of his own breath and the hammering of his heart. Then he saw the glow of a lantern going slowly to and fro amongst the high walls and buildings, as though someone were searching, and he drew himself deeper into the darkness. But the light didn't come any closer, and after a while he couldn't see it any more.

'Katta?' he called in a barely audible whisper, and then again, scared lest anyone but her should hear him. But no one answered.

It wasn't until dawn that he dared crawl from his hiding place. Cautiously he stood up and looked around. A low mist had rolled in across the ice, filling the hollow places amongst the ruins, drifting between the fallen walls.

He didn't know what to do.

Then, deadened by the mist, he heard the sound of voices, only faintly at first. He drew himself back into the wall and listened. Someone was calling his name.

Koenig had already found Stefan. Now he was searching for Katta and Mathias. As he stepped out of the mist in front of Mathias, he looked like a dead man. For one moment that's what Mathias thought he was. His face was ash-grey, his lips bloodless. He stood looking at Mathias with hollow-set eyes.

'Where is Katta?' he said.

Mathias shook his head. A little way behind Koenig, Stefan walked out of the mist.

'She was with you,' Mathias said.

'She run.'

Stefan made a movement with his arm as though to show that she'd gone another way and that he'd lost her. But he did it as though he were not quite sure which way that was.

They began to search among the ruins, calling her name, but she didn't answer and they didn't find her.

It was only as the mist blew away and they stood on the cliff top, looking down onto the rocks below, that they saw the two sets of tracks left by the runners of a sleigh. One set curving out across the ice towards them, and the other going back towards the land.

25

The Drum-shaped Room

Katta woke.

She was lying on a hard cold floor. Her wrists were tied together with a cord. There was a bitter-sick taste in her mouth. It was the lingering taste of the cloth that Dr Leiter had held over her face, pushing it so tightly against her that she couldn't breathe in anything else. She remembered struggling against it and her head filling with screaming, then velvet-black silence.

Now she was here, but she didn't know where 'here' was. Blinking slowly, she looked around.

She was in a large room. It had a high, gilded ceiling. Rows of cages hung along its walls. Some held small birds that flitted from perch to perch; others had squirrels, others cats. In one a small monkey sat watching her. Row upon row of sharp, beady eyes all watching her. There were tables too, but she couldn't see onto them.

Voices were coming from another room. Getting closer. What she had taken to be a grand bookcase set into the wall suddenly swung open and a man stepped through. She didn't know him, but the man who came behind him was Dr Leiter.

'She should be awake,' Leiter was saying, but there was hesitation in his voice as he said the words, as though he were worried what the consequence might be if he were wrong.

The other man wore a long thick gown trimmed with rich fur. He was older than Leiter and was carrying Katta's leather cap in one hand. Instinctively she tried to put her hands to her head, feeling for it.

'Will it make any difference?' he said to Leiter.

'No,' said Leiter. 'I examined her while she slept. She is fit and strong. It was some accident perhaps, no more than that.'

And Katta heard it again, that same uncertainty. It took her a moment to understand what it was, and then she realized.

Leiter was afraid.

'Good,' said the man.

He stood looking down at her with pale green eyes, and then she felt it too – cold clawing fear. It didn't need words; it was wrapped about this man like a cloak.

'I hope you are pleased with her, Toymaker,' said Leiter.

'She is the right height too,' the Toymaker said.

Katta felt her mouth moving before she even knew what it was she was going to say. She could feel the inside of her palms damp with fear.

'My friends know I'm here,' she blurted out.

Menschenmacher might not have heard her. He reached down and began parting her hair with his fingertips, looking for the small broken place on her head. She tried to move her head away, but he wound her hair around his other hand and pulled it so tight that she couldn't move. Then, with a touch full of menace, he ran his fingernail around the edges of the bone. Katta let out a whimper.

'Did you look in the coffins?' he said.

'No!' she gasped.

He dug his fingernail under the edge of the bone. It felt like hot wire. Her breath came in short, terrified gasps.

'Did you?'

321

'Yes!'

'What did you see?'

'The Duke!' She couldn't say the words quickly enough – she just wanted him to stop.

'Who else saw him? Your friends?'

'Yes!'

'Does anyone else know?'

'No!'

He looked up at Leiter. 'She is the only one left?'

Leiter nodded.

He let go of her hair. She tried to scrabble away from him, but her hands were tied.

'I don't know nothin',' she whimpered. 'Please?'

She looked imploringly at Leiter, as though, of all people, he might help her. But his face was impassive.

'Bring her,' the Toymaker said.

Leiter reached down and lifted Katta to her feet. She stood up, mute and terrified. He put one arm around her shoulders, like some kindly old uncle, and together they followed the other man.

They went between the tables. The tops were covered in things that she didn't understand at all – tools, lathes, tiny wheels and cogs. On a slab of clean white porcelain lay a little marmoset monkey; its

unseeing milk-glazed eyes were turned towards her. Its chest had been cut open and the fur hooked back with long silver pins. She looked quickly away.

'We won't hurt you,' said Leiter, but she could feel his hand on her back, gently pushing her forward.

They went through another door and into a room, round like a clean, white drum. Daylight flooded through a domed ceiling of clear glass. Katta could see clouds and the blue, wintry sky beyond.

In front of her were two large tables. One was scrubbed clean and laid out with tools and sharp instruments. Motionless on the other was a young woman in a pale cotton gown. Leiter pushed Katta forward and closed the door. It shut with a click behind them.

The Toymaker turned and looked at her. 'Give the girl a drink, Leiter,' he said.

Unhurriedly Leiter filled a small glass from a jug on the table. It took him a moment and he had his back to Katta as he did it. When he turned round, he held the glass out to her. She stared at the glass, then at him.

'It is only water,' he said. 'Drink it.'

She took the glass in both hands, then, like a small

child told to take medicine, she put it to her lips and drank, watching Leiter the whole time. Her hands were shaking, but her mouth was so dry. He took the empty glass from her.

'Now, come and see,' said the Toymaker.

He was standing beside the young woman, lightly brushing her hair with his hand.

Katta moved closer, and then stopped. Sleeping people breathe; they move – you only have to look carefully enough and you see it. But the young woman on the table wasn't breathing at all. She wasn't dead either – dead people look dead, like Jacob, but she didn't.

Katta looked up at him, not knowing what she was supposed to do.

'Touch her,' he said.

Hesitantly she reached out a hand and touched the tips of her fingers against the young woman's cheek. As she did so, Katta's face clouded with confusion and she pulled her hand back, because the skin was hard and cold. She wasn't real at all.

She was a doll.

'All she needs is a heart, child. When she has a heart, even you would believe that she was real. She will be able to dance and talk, though she will never need to say very many words. Her beauty will speak for her.'

Katta looked at the face of the young woman and it seemed to her that she was seeing something she'd seen before – the cold, empty face of the Duke as he had walked beneath her window. She was just like him.

'You see,' the Toymaker said, 'the people expect their Duke to take a wife.'

As he spoke, he picked up from the table a small fine ivory handle. There was nothing else to it that Katta could see.

'All she needs,' he said, 'is a heart.'

Katta could hear his voice. She could see him holding the thin ivory handle in his hand, but the room was wider than it had been a moment before. It felt as if she were watching what was happening, without being part of it at all. She turned round and looked at Leiter. He was still holding the empty glass, but he was watching her as though he had been waiting for this. He put the glass on the table and she knew that it couldn't just have been water. He caught her as her legs gave way, holding her as she slowly folded to the floor.

The Toymaker's voice came slowly, out of a fog a

thousand miles away. 'Even my little dolls with sparrows' hearts sometimes remember they were sparrows, once. You will have to tell me, Duchess, if you ever remember being a girl.'

A line of bloody footprints marked the path that Koenig took as they came back across the ice. He walked slowly, his fist pressed deep into the wound made by Valter's knife, but still it bled. None of them spoke. Mathias watched Koenig, expecting him to fall at any moment, but he didn't. He just kept on walking, step by step, his eyes fixed on the distant shoreline as though that was all he could see.

Stefan walked on the other side of him. Every now and again he would cast a glance at Mathias. He didn't know whether Mathias had guessed that he'd left Katta behind. All the time they'd spent looking for her on the island, Stefan had hidden what he'd done, not knowing what to do if he found her first. He didn't know what to do now either – Koenig was bleeding to death, he could see it, and he didn't know what to do.

Still Koenig walked on, step by step, fist pressed into the wound, his eyes never leaving the distant shore.

Mathias hadn't understood exactly what they had found in the crypt, but he knew now that Gustav's secret wasn't gold or silver – it was murder. What Katta had said made no sense to him. He wasn't sure if he'd even heard it right – how could those men have been dead and still alive? And where was she? He looked at Koenig, at the blood seeping into the ice, and such a wave of despair welled up in him that he buried his face in his hands and began to cry.

But still Koenig walked on.

When at last they reached the harbour, they made their way between the tangle of thick ropes, and up across the quay to the stables. If there were stable-boys about, none saw them. In the warm dark of the stall, Koenig stood with his eyes closed, resting his forehead against the side of the huge horse. Then he turned his head and looked at the square of daylight that fell through the door.

'Get me that coat,' he said.

A dirty stable coat hung on a nail. It must have belonged to one of the grooms. Stefan pulled it down and watched as, one-handed, Koenig slowly unbuttoned the blood-sodden remains of the coat he wore and dropped it onto the straw. Then he began to wash himself clean in the ice-cold water of the drinking trough. He unwound his fine lace scarf and stuffed it into the deep wound that Valter had made, binding it tight. But it did little good. It stained with blood even as he did it.

'We have to get you to a doctor,' said Mathias.

Koenig shook his head. 'The little man was meant to kill us,' he said. 'Leiter doesn't know that he didn't.'

It was only then that Mathias understood what Koenig meant to do. He had an account to settle with Leiter. Katta was a small part of it, but if she were alive, Koenig would find her. That was all that mattered to Mathias. He didn't care about the rest.

'Thank you,' he said.

Koenig pulled the remaining pistol from the bags beneath the straw. 'Don't thank me yet, boy,' he said.

Koenig knew where they had to go, just as Anna-Maria and Lutsmann had done. No one spared them a look as they pushed their way through the streets. The narrow lanes and alleyways were full of carts and stalls. Mathias looked at the faces they passed, wanting to find one that was Katta's. But they passed only one red-haired girl, and when she turned round, she looked straight through him.

Dr Leiter's house stood in one of the courtyards of the palace. There were no guards or soldiers – not there. Leiter had no need of them.

The building had a fine front and a walled garden at the rear. There was a door in the wall that wasn't locked. They pushed it open and stood under the bare trees, looking up at the back of the house. A low frost-covered hedge ran beside a path that led to windows opening onto the garden.

If Leiter had been careless about the door in the wall, he hadn't been careless about the windows. Each one was bolted shut.

Koenig said something to Stefan that Mathias didn't understand. Stefan took his knife from inside his coat and, with the tip of the blade, began to peel back the line of soft lead that set the little panes of glass in the frame. His hand was shaking as he worked.

Before he'd finished, they had to drop below the line of the window as a housemaid came into the room. She passed right above them, but she didn't see the small missing pieces of glass that Stefan had already loosened. They waited, listening for sounds of alarm, but none came. Stefan loosened one more square, then, reaching his arm through the hole he had made, slipped the bolt and pushed the window open.

Koenig rested his back against the wall, his eyes momentarily closed, his teeth gritted. Mathias could see fresh wet blood on his hand where he had walked with it pressed beneath the coat.

He opened his eyes. 'Come,' he said, and pulled himself through the window.

The room was empty. They crossed to the door and opened it a crack. Outside was a galleried hall with a wide staircase, portraits on the wall and a glass chandelier on its gilded chain – it was the place where Lutsmann and Anna-Maria had waited. It was empty too.

'Up,' said Koenig.

Slipping quietly through the door, they began to climb the stairs. But as they reached the top, a man carrying a large sheaf of papers stepped backwards out of a room in front of them. He didn't see them. The papers were slipping from his hands and he was preoccupied with them. Then he turned his head.

'Who are you?' he said.

'Herr Doctor Leiter told me to come to him here,' said Koenig.

'I know nothing of this,' said the man. 'What does he want with you?'

'That is Herr Doctor Leiter's business,' said Koenig.

The man drew himself up. 'I am Doctor Leiter's secretary,' he said.

'Then, Mister Secretary,' said Koenig, 'take me to his rooms.'

This time the man's face darkened. 'You have to wait for him downstairs,' he said.

'No,' said Koenig, pulling the pistol from his coat. 'We wait for him in his rooms.'

The man could see the blood on Koenig's hand. He could see how unsteady the pistol was in it. But if he had thought to shout out, then Koenig had seen that too.

'Even I could not miss you from here, Mister Secretary,' he said.

The man's mouth opened and closed. Still holding the papers, he turned round and, with Koenig a step behind him, began to walk back towards the door that he had just come through. When he reached it, he stopped.

'Open it,' said Koenig.

They were two steps into the room when Koenig

hit him with the butt of the pistol. There was a sound like the crack of bone and the man dropped like a sack.

'Get him out of sight,' said Koenig.

Stefan dragged the man behind a chair, but Mathias stood dumbly in the doorway, staring at the sudden violence of it. Koenig pulled him inside and pushed the door shut.

'Now we wait for Leiter,' he said.

He walked across to Leiter's desk. It was strewn with letters and papers. He looked at them for a moment, then came and stood behind the door with his back against the wall and closed his eyes.

Mathias listened to the silence of the room. It was almost unbearable. Above the fireplace the clock ticked. It struck the quarter, then the half-hour. Its little bells were still ringing, as from somewhere downstairs in the house came the sound of a heavy door closing. Koenig opened his eyes. They could hear footsteps coming unhurriedly up the hard marble stairs. There was Leiter's voice too, sharp and ill-tempered.

'Have him come up to me when you find him,' he was saying.

Mathias guessed it was the secretary that Leiter

wanted. He could just see the tips of the man's feet behind a chair – Leiter would see them too – but before he could say anything, the handle of the door twitched, and it opened.

Leiter didn't bother to close it. He was dressed in his dark tailcoat. He walked across to the desk, dropped the silver-topped cane across it and, picking up one of the letters, then another, began reading. Then something on the desk caught his eye. He stopped reading and slowly touched a fingertip to what he had seen. Rubbing it between finger and thumb, he held it up to the light.

It was blood.

He slowly straightened as he put down the letters while, behind him, Koenig pushed the door closed.

26

The Duchess

Leiter didn't turn round at once. As though curious to see what would happen, he reached his hand towards the small silver bell on the table.

'You would be dead before anyone came,' said Koenig quietly.

Leiter still didn't turn round, but he hesitated, his hand just above the bell. 'But they would still come,' he said.

'And you would still be dead,' said Koenig.

Leiter didn't move. 'Then we are at an impasse,' he said.

He lifted his hand away from the bell and only then turned round.

Koenig stood next to the door with his back to the wall. His face was sunken and full of pain. He held the pistol cradled across his chest. The hand that held it was wet with blood. Mathias stood beside him.

'But I am looking at a dead man,' said Leiter calmly, as though he were being shown a curiosity that puzzled him. 'Valter is usually much more thorough than this. I will need to speak to him when I have done with you.' His eyes rested momentarily on the pistol that Koenig held. 'I wonder if you even have enough strength to pull the trigger,' he said.

Koenig didn't answer, but with a click, loud in the silence of the room, he drew the pistol hammer back with his thumb.

Leiter smiled.

Mathias saw it all. It was like watching a cat and a mouse. But there was no telling which was which.

'What is it that you want?' said Leiter. 'To rob me?'

He held his hands out to the room, and it was only in half turning round as he did so that he saw Stefan.

'Another?' He looked back at Koenig. 'What you see is all there is,' he said. 'Take.'

But Koenig didn't move.

'Or perhaps you want something else?' said Leiter.

'The girl,' said Mathias. 'Where's Katta?'

Leiter didn't even bother to look at him. He was watching Koenig.

'How did the conjuror know?' said Koenig slowly.

Even those few words were an effort, and Leiter could see it. He didn't answer straight away. He watched Koenig's face.

'He was in the palace,' he said at last. 'It was a whim of the Duke, to see a conjuror – he was not well enough to travel. Only the conjuror went wandering where he should not have wandered, saw what he should not have seen.'

'Two dukes,' said Koenig.

'Two dukes,' agreed Leiter. 'But, inconveniently, one of them had just had his throat cut.'

'By you,' said Koenig.

Leiter inclined his head, as though reluctantly accepting praise. 'By me,' he said. 'It is a physician's skill. But I only did what I was asked to do.'

'And now you have a puppet duke,' said Koenig.

Then Leiter laughed. He laughed as though what Koenig had said had been unintentionally but immeasurably funny. Mathias couldn't understand why, but Leiter laughed.

'Oh, much better than a puppet duke, Burner man,' he said. 'You might even say "good as a little toy". A little toy duke and a little toy bishop. You can play games with them, you see – they do whatever you tell them. Can you even begin to know how much power that is to have, Burner man?'

'Too much to let a conjuror spoil,' said Koenig.

'Too much to let a conjuror spoil,' said Leiter. 'It took us a long time to find him, but we found him in the end. And now,' he said, the smile dying on his lips, 'there is just you.'

'And the girl,' said Koenig.

'But of course,' said Leiter silkily. 'How could I forget the girl?'

'Give me the girl,' said Koenig. 'You can keep the rest.'

Leiter looked at him coldly. 'That is a very handsome offer to make,' he said. 'But can I believe you?'

Koenig pointed the pistol at Leiter's heart. 'You don't have any choice,' he said.

Leiter smiled again.

Cat and mouse.

'Very well,' he said.

The door in the panelled wall of Leiter's room, the one that Valter had come through, opened onto a flight of stone steps and a long passage. Leiter went first, a lantern in his hand. Koenig walked behind him with the pistol at Leiter's back. There were

338

darker openings to the right and the left, but Leiter walked past each one. The passage was damp and cold. Every now and then he would stop and, turning round, hold the lantern up so that he could see Koenig's face – see how much more blood he had lost, how much strength he had left. Each time, as though more satisfied with what he saw, he would turn away and walk steadily on.

'I hope I am not going too fast for you, Burner man,' he said.

The palms of Mathias's hands were wet with fear. He walked beside Koenig in the shadow of the lantern, watching the black-coated back of Leiter. Stefan walked half a step away from him. Sometimes the two boys glanced at each other, but they didn't speak. They didn't need any words. They each knew that Leiter wouldn't let them live, and they knew, just as surely, that Koenig was going to kill him.

And Leiter knew it too.

At the end of the passage a few steps led up towards another door. It was bolted shut. At the top of the steps Leiter put the lantern down, slid the bolt and, pushing the door open, led them through into the bright, cold daylight of the drum-shaped room. For a moment Mathias was dazzled by the light.

Then he saw her, lying on the scrubbed table, half covered with a stained sheet. Her mouth was open as though she were about to speak, but her eyes were glazed and unseeing, staring up at the glass roof and the cold winter sky.

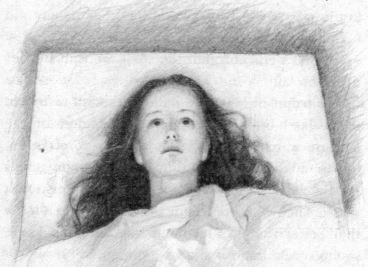

He shouted her name. In his confusion he pulled at Koenig's arm. Koenig stumbled, and that was enough for Leiter. In an instant he had snatched a short blade from the cuff of his coat. But it wasn't Koenig that he took. There was someone else much nearer. Leiter had stepped aside as they came into the room, and Stefan had been last through the door. Maybe he'd held back. Maybe he had been too scared to go on. But in one quick movement Leiter had pressed the sharp steel to Stefan's throat, and with an arm round his neck, dragged Stefan backwards through the door. Before Koenig could do a thing, Leiter had slammed it shut and slid the bolt fast.

Koenig hammered at the closed door, but it wouldn't open. Through the thick wood of it they heard Stefan cry out, but the cry was cut short by a horrible choking, like a sheep coughing in a field at night. Then there was nothing. As Mathias watched, a single thread of blood wound slowly through the gap beneath the door, pushing the dust and grit of the floor in front of it as it went. Then Koenig saw it too. He shouted out Stefan's name, beating on the door as hard as he could, but no answer came. In the silence that followed they heard the sound of Leiter's fading footsteps, unhurried along the dark passage.

Koenig, his strength all but spent, leaned his head against the door and shut his eyes. Then Mathias saw that there were tears on his face. He was saying Stefan's name and silently crying.

Mathias stared dumbly, and then suddenly it all

made sense – Koenig and Stefan. Why had he never seen it before?

He made himself turn round and look at Katta again, but there was no mistaking that she was dead. It felt like the end of everything.

As he stood looking at her, Koenig stepped away from the door and moved him aside. Leaning over Katta, he felt for the pulse in her neck, but there wasn't one. He brushed away the strands of hair that had fallen across her face, then closed her mouth and her eyes.

Mathias felt sick. He couldn't look any more. He turned away. There was a noise clamouring inside his head. It sounded like a bell. It was only slowly that he realized it *was* a bell. A real bell. Somewhere, someone had begun to ring a bell. He looked up at Koenig with alarm.

'They're coming,' he said.

But Koenig couldn't answer. He was leaning against the table, his hand pressed to the wound that Valter had made. His breath was thin and shallow. When he lifted his face to Mathias, the eyes that looked out were leaden. He shook his head.

'Let them come,' he said.

'No!' said Mathias.

Something lit inside him. He wasn't going to die like Katta or Stefan. Not here. Not like this.

He put his arm around Koenig and, gritting his teeth against the grating of bone in his chest, he pulled him towards the only other door. It was the one that Katta had come through. It wasn't locked. The room beyond it was just as she'd seen it when she woke – half-made, half-finished things, awaiting hearts. It was an awful place. Mathias tried to make Koenig move faster, but Koenig could only manage creeping steps. As Mathias tried to pull him on, Koenig pushed his hand away. In a voice little more than a whisper, he said something that Mathias didn't hear. With a huge effort, he said the words again.

'Burn it. Burn it all.'

Then Mathias understood.

He began sweeping the tabletops clear, smashing every spirit jar and bottle onto the floor. He pulled a curtain from its hanging, and trod it into the wet mess that he'd made. Then he stood back and watched. Koenig covered the pan of the pistol, and struck the flint. A single spark curved and fell, and with a thump, like the shaking of a huge blanket, the soaked floor caught fire.

The flames took hold with astonishing speed. They curved up the walls and across the beams of the gilded ceiling. In the cages, the birds and animals began flapping and beating against the bars, hissing and screeching. But Mathias didn't see them any more than he heard the roar of the fire, because he had suddenly realized something more awful than that.

There was no door.

The room was filling with stinging smoke. A tapestry on the wall burst into flame, burning like dry paper. A row of spirit jars fell and smashed as the shelf they stood on caught fire. Mathias could feel the sudden heat of the flames blistering his skin.

But there was no door, only the one they had come through, and that was lost to them on the other side of the fire. With a crash, one of the huge windows shattered and the fire shot greedily upwards and out.

There had to be a door, hidden like the one in Leiter's panelled room. They began pulling at the books and shelves on the wall.

But there was no door.

And then they found it, a lock plate where there needn't have been one. They could see the join in the wall. Koenig pulled at it, beat weakly at the lock with the butt of the pistol, but it wouldn't move. So he stepped back, put the muzzle to the place and fired. Shards of metal sang past their ears as the lock burst. Coughing and choking, they pulled at it and fell through the door into the room beyond.

It was a galleried hall with stairs at either end. The air about them was filling with smoke. Above the roar of the fire they could hear men shouting. Mathias looked about, not sure what to do.

'Up,' hissed Koenig. His teeth were gritted, his face creased with pain. 'Up,' he said.

Together they stumbled towards the stairs. They had only just reached the top when men spilled out into the hall below them, but not one of them looked up. All they could see was the fire. They threw off their coats and jackets and began beating at the flames, shouting for water and buckets. But the floor beneath their feet was already alight.

Mathias didn't wait to see. Pulling Koenig after him, he started along the gallery, not knowing where he was going. Another bell was ringing now, louder than the first, more clamorous, as the smell of smoke and burning filled the air. There were shouts and voices too. As they turned one corner, people pushed past them, running, but no one stopped them. Mathias had no idea where they were. The place was a labyrinth. Koenig could go no further. He folded to his knees and closed his eyes.

They were by a high window that opened onto a terrace. From it, Mathias could see where the fire had taken hold. Huge flames had already broken through the roof of the palace. Thick smoke was billowing upwards. In the courtyard below, people were running to and fro, but there was no way of fighting the fire. The water in the troughs and fountains was frozen solid.

'Come on!' said Mathias, pulling at Koenig. 'Get up!' He tried to lift him to his feet, but he couldn't. 'Get up!'

'I don't think he can,' said a voice behind him.

Mathias didn't need to turn round to know whose it was.

Leiter was standing at the end of the passage, the silver-topped cane in his hand. But he wasn't alone. A young woman in a plain gown stood beside him. Her face was cold and hard.

Koenig still held the empty pistol in his hand. Mathias pulled it from his grasp.

'I'll shoot you!' he said.

'Will you really?' said Leiter and began to walk towards him.

'Stay back!'

The pistol was heavy and awkward. Mathias pulled back the hammer and pointed it at Leiter's chest, praying that something would happen, but the hammer only fell with an empty click when he pulled the trigger, just as he knew it would.

With a look of amusement on his face, Leiter turned towards the woman. 'We have found them, Duchess,' he said. 'Would you like to play a game now?'

She looked at him, her face furrowing as she tried to follow his words. Then, slowly, she nodded her head.

'But these are not our friends, are they?'

Just as slowly, she shook her head, as though she hadn't known that before.

'Shall we kill them?' said Leiter. 'That would be a good game.'

She turned her head and looked at Mathias and Koenig.

Leiter twisted the silver handle and drew the long sharp blade from the cane. 'Would you like to kill them?' he said, his voice singsong, as though talking to a small child.

She looked at him, slowly following the words, then she nodded.

He held the blade out to her, and she took it from him.

'No,' said Mathias.

He tried desperately to make Koenig stand, but he couldn't. Koenig just raised his eyes and, through a sea of pain, watched as she walked slowly towards them. There was nothing he could do.

Mathias looked up at her, pleading. 'Please?' he said.

She stared down at him, hard-faced, but then her face clouded as though something had suddenly puzzled her. She frowned. Slowly she turned and looked at Leiter. He hadn't moved. He was watching her.

'Kill them, Duchess,' he said.

But she hesitated. She looked down at the man, and at the boy. Then her lips moved as though she were trying to say something.

'Kill them,' said Leiter.

She lifted the blade and Mathias flinched from her, his eyes tight shut. He didn't see her take the two quick steps and drive the steel straight through Leiter's heart. Eyes bulging with astonishment,

Leiter stood, his mouth rounded in a perfect, silent O. He looked down at the blade in his chest, and as he did so, a stain like the bloom of a rose spread across the front of his white shirt. Without taking her eyes from him, she pushed in the blade right to its silver handle, and only then did she let go, watching him as he sank slowly to the floor at her feet.

Even little dolls with sparrows' hearts sometimes remember they were sparrows once.

As Mathias opened his eyes, she was standing quite still, her fingers lightly touching her cheek as though brushing it with a feather that had dropped from a carnival mask.

In a voice that he never thought to hear again – haltingly, uncertainly – she said her name.

27
Last Steps

Mathias could still hear the shouts of alarm, smell the bitter stinging smoke that filled the air. But suddenly it all seemed far away. Dumbly he stood up.

Leiter lay dead on the floor at the woman's feet – his eyes were wide open, the silver-topped cane driven straight through his heart. She was standing over him, but she wasn't looking at him. She was holding her hands in front of her face, staring at them as though she'd never seen them before. Even as he watched her, she put them hesitantly to her head, feeling for something that should be there and wasn't.

And then she screamed.

She screamed as though every demon in hell had found her.

He started to back away, but she was too quick.

She caught hold of him, her eyes staring and mad. Her grip was like iron.

'Like – them!' she cried.

And for Mathias the world stopped – it was Katta's voice that he heard coming from her mouth. Broken and mad, but Katta's voice, as though somehow she were locked inside.

She saw the look of blank incomprehension register on his face. 'Yes! Like – them!' she said, nodding insanely.

He felt her fingers wrap in his; they were hard and cold. She pressed his hand to her cheek. It was hard and cold too, like a doll. Her eyes never leaving his, she put his hand to her breast. It was hard and cold, but he could feel a heart beating beneath.

'My – heart!' she gasped. 'Mmm-eeee!'

The words made no sense. For Mathias it was just as it had been for Katta in the crypt when she saw the dead men that she knew were alive – and suddenly the two moments connected in his mind and he realized what she was trying to say.

She was like them.

And then he knew why Leiter had laughed.

This is what Gustav really knew.

They weren't men at all.

351

She could see him staring at her in disbelief – his face, the hall and the smoke – but for her it was like looking through thick windows at a world outside. She couldn't even say the words she wanted. They were drowned by the deafening whine, like wasps in her head, of a thousand minute cogs and wheels as they wound and turned – and through it all, pounding like a drum, she could hear the hammer beat of her own heart.

Only one word came, and it sounded like a scream.

'Mmeee!'

What happened next happened like a slow nightmare.

There were flames on the stairs behind them. Koenig lay folded against the wall where he'd fallen. Mathias couldn't see whether he was alive or dead, but with Katta's help he lifted him to his feet. They half walked, half dragged him through the window and onto the terrace outside.

The palace was ablaze.

Flames had leaped unchecked from building to building, and now it was all on fire. People were running and shouting – horses let free from the burning stables ran amok between them. Everywhere was smoke and burning and noise.

There was a long ornate stair that wound down from the terrace into the gardens below. Holding Koenig between them, they went down it step by step.

No one stopped them. No one questioned them. They pushed through the press of people and no one spared them a look – not at the gates, not in the streets or in the alleys. There were only eyes for the soaring flames and the bright hot embers that carried on the wind and drifted out over the frost-covered roofs of the city below.

Sometimes it seemed that she knew who she was; sometimes she didn't. She'd put her hands to her head and scream, and then there was nothing that Mathias could do.

At last they reached the stable. It was dark now – an eerie, flame-lit dark with shadows that moved.

Mathias laid Koenig in the straw. For a moment in that darkness, the bloodless face looked like Gustav's had done all that time before.

'We have to get him help,' said Mathias, but Katta didn't answer.

She was crouching in the straw, rocking to and fro,

her hands to her head, trying to shut out the noise that was driving her insane. He didn't understand that though. All he could see was the mad woman rocking in the dirty straw.

He didn't know what to do. He felt the world swim as the hopeless enormity of it all overwhelmed him.

Then, in the flickering of the light that fell on the wall, he saw the saddle.

Somewhere in the woods nearby there had to be Burners. If he could only find them, they would help. They would know what to do.

Looking at the mad woman and the dying man, he pulled the saddle from the wall. He heaved it across the back of the horse. It turned its head and he saw the angry white of its eye, but he didn't care. Fumbling beneath its belly for the strap, he drew the buckle up as tightly as he could, then he bent over Koenig and shook him. Slowly, as though being called from a long way away, Koenig opened his eyes.

'Can you ride?' said Mathias, his face pressed close to Koenig's. 'You have to ride.'

If you had stood at the city gates, you might have seen them – a boy leading a huge horse by the rein

– a grim, silent man in the saddle and a mad woman walking beside him, her hand upon his stirrup.

But you wouldn't have looked.

You would only have had eyes for the fire – for the huge columns of flame and sparks that engulfed the top of the hill.

No.

You wouldn't have seen them.

And the boy didn't look back.

Epilogue

In the spring, the ice in the harbour melts. The floes break up and drift out to sea.

When it does, some people might take a boat out to the islands to visit the monastery of St Becca the Old. They might walk between its ruined walls or sit on the rough grass and listen to the thump of the sea against the rocks below.

They might even go into the chapel itself.

But they will find nothing.

The stairs to the crypt have been filled in and covered. Even the floor has been swept quite clean, though there is a dark stain on the stones that might have been blood.

And of Valter? Of the thousand minute wheels and cogs that filled his head?

If they looked for him?

They would find not a trace.

ACKNOWLEDGEMENTS

I would like to thank Linda Sargent for her unfailing encouragement and friendship over more years than I care to name, and David Fickling, Bella Pearson and Ben Sharpe who between them helped me make this a better story than I would have made of it alone.

This story was begun for the children of Wells Central Junior School, Somerset, in the school year 2005 to 2006. My thanks go to them and also to Jane Murray whose idea it was that I should come to the school, and to Mike Rossiter, my friend and supporter while I was there.

SHADOW FOREST

BY MATT HAIG

Samuel Blink is the hero of this story, but he doesn't
know it yet. Right now, he and his sister Martha are
in the back of his parents' car. He has no idea a giant
log is about to fall from the sky and change his life
for ever. He doesn't know that he and Martha will be
forced to move to Norway and eat their Aunt Eda's
smelly brown cheese. He hasn't the slightest clue
Martha will disappear into Shadow Forest. A forest
full of one-eyed trolls, the sinister huldre-folk,
deadly truth pixies and a witch who steals shadows.
A forest ruled by the evil Changemaker. A forest so
dangerous that people who enter never return.

No Samuel Blink doesn't know any of this.
So don't tell him. It might ruin the book . . .

BLUE PETER BOOK AWARD WINNER
NESTLÉ CHILDREN'S BOOK PRIZE GOLD
AWARD WINNER

978 0 552 55563 0

THE RUNAWAY TROLL

BY MATT HAIG

Samuel Blink's list of what NOT to do if you're
bored in Norway (and don't want to eat any
more of Aunt Eda's smelly brown cheese):

1. Find a one-eyed troll under your bed

2. Hide the troll in your wardrobe

3. If anyone asks, lie about why there is a smell
of cabbage coming from your room

4. Attract the attention of the most evil troll
in Shadow Forest, the Betterer

5. Get kidnapped

6. Rely on your ten-year-old sister to
save you . . .

978 0 370 32988 8

INTO THE WOODS

BY LYN GARDNER

Aurora Eden's List of VERY Important Things to do Today

1. Tell Storm off for making fireworks – AGAIN!

2. Bake chocolate-coated madeleines.

3. Dust behind the kitchen cabinets – IMPORTANT!

4. Ask Storm if she knows anything about that funny-looking musical pipe I found behind the pickle jars.

5. See if Desdemona has laid any eggs.

6. Set Storm ESPECIALLY hard maths test as punishment for crying WOLF.

7. Make sure no one finds out we are living without a Grown-up.

8. Convince Storm that Witches Aren't Real.
9. Rearrange linen cupboard.

10. DON'T GO INTO THE WOODS!

978 0 552 55459 6

OUT OF THE WOODS

BY LYN GARDNER

ROLL UP!
ROLL UP! ROLL UP! ROLL UP!

THE WORLD'S MOST
ASTONISHING FUN-FAIR

Free rides and candy floss for ~~children~~
almost-orphans and those of
EXCEPTIONAL beauty

978 0 385 61036 0